SECOND CHANCES

Andi McWhorter

CROSSBOOKS
PUBLISHING

CrossBooks™
1663 Liberty Drive
Bloomington, IN 47403
www.crossbooks.com
Phone: 1-866-879-0502

©2009 Andi McWhorter. All rights reserved.

No part of this book may be reproduced, stored in a retrieval system, or transmitted by any means without the written permission of the author.

First published by CrossBooks 12/16/2009

ISBN: 978-1-6150-7041-1 (sc)
ISBN 978-1-6150-7125-8 (hc)

Library of Congress Control Number: 2009912911

Printed in the United States of America
Bloomington, Indiana

This book is printed on acid-free paper.

DEDICATION:

To Sumner, Jarrett, and MacKenzie – God blessed me more than I ever deserved when He gave me the three of you. You make me so proud! I love you more every day!

To Ricky – You make our life the fairy tale I used to dream about so long ago. Thank you for believing in second chances, romance, faith, and family -- but, most of all, for believing in me. I love you.

In memory of my loving grandparents, Robert "RocRoc" and Margie "MeMa" Coley

SUMMARY

After the untimely death of his father, young Luke Garrison sets out on a summer adventure that will ultimately change his life. Unable to cope amidst all the daily reminders on his parents' Montana ranch, Luke heads to his aunt and uncle's for the summer with one goal in mind—to get over his father's death and move on with his life. The last thing on his mind is meeting the girl of his dreams.

Emily Alderman, with her mysterious past and well-kept secrets, is someone with whom Luke is immediately captivated. And against her better judgment, Emily is drawn to Luke, too. But before Luke can convince Emily that they share something special, he has to persuade her that he, unlike any other man in her life, can be trusted. And Emily finds that she has her own challenges to deal with as far as Luke is concerned when she tries to show him that life is more than just bad things happening to decent people, and that losing someone you love is far better than never having loved anyone at all.

As the two eventually develop a relationship, they not only discover each other's secrets but also learn some very valuable lessons along the way. Most importantly, they learn that no matter what life throws you, somewhere along the line, if you're lucky, life gives you second chances.

CHAPTER ONE

As the blue Ford pickup truck headed out of town, the sky began to turn an ugly, dark gray, and for the first time that morning, it looked as if rain would be inevitable. The country-and-western song playing on the radio was interrupted as a news bulletin declared, "A severe thunderstorm is rapidly approaching our listening area. Golf-ball-sized hail has been reported, and all listeners are being warned to stay indoors until this storm system passes through. Stay tuned to this station for the latest information and updates."

"Well, there go my plans!" Luke Garrison grumbled. He'd been looking forward to a Saturday afternoon fishing trip for quite some time, and now he had no idea when he would get another chance. Not that he didn't have a lot of free time on his hands. After his kids grew up and married, all Luke had focused on were his wife, Sarah, and their thousand-acre Montana ranch. But then, after a long bout with cancer last year, Sarah had finally passed away, leaving him with only Will and Jake, the two ranch hands, to keep him company. And really, the two of them easily managed the ranch without Luke's help, but ranching was the only thing that seemed to pass the time for him now.

As he pulled the truck into the dirt driveway, Luke gazed over his homeland. *So many memories,* he thought, *funny how life turns out so different than what you plan.* Will's wife, Nell, was waiting on the porch for Luke as he handed her the little bit of groceries he had brought back from the store. Nell helped out around the house some and cooked lunch for the three working men each day.

"Sounds like a nasty one coming, huh?" asked Nell, more to make conversation than anything else.

Luke, not really up for talking, said, "Um, that's what they say." He took the cold glass of tea Nell had fixed for him and decided to sit on the porch for a while before the storm hit. Nell headed inside to put away the groceries.

As he closed his eyes and began to relax, Luke said to himself, "Yep, funny how life turns out." With that one statement, the memories began to take over—memories Luke had tried hard to bury, although his very soul refused to let him; memories of a summer more than thirty years ago, when he was eighteen years old and fresh out of high school; memories of someone he had tried so desperately to forget. Looking back over his life, one could actually be fooled into believing he had forgotten about her—but it wasn't that simple. It had all been too real to ever forget.

CHAPTER TWO

It was a frost-covered Monday morning the day young Luke headed into town, eager to pick up his newly tailored black suit for graduation that night. It had been a long winter in Bozeman, and even now in May, the mornings could get pretty chilly before the sun rose into full view. Luke couldn't help but whistle as he headed into the men's store, anxious to get this whole day over with as quickly as possible. School had never been one of his favorite things; helping his dad on the ranch and taking time to fish and hunt had always seemed like much better options to him over the years. But, because it had meant so much to his parents, mainly because neither of them had completed high school, Luke had toughed it out and was quite proud of himself for doing so. Now, with school behind him, he could go on and begin taking over the ranch for his father. Being the only child, he looked at the ranch as not only his responsibility, but more important, his livelihood.

If Luke's parents could have changed things, they would have. Logan and Caroline didn't marry until they were both in their late twenties, but in order to establish themselves and their home, they had quickly decided to wait awhile before attempting to have children. They were both hardworking individuals, and since Logan's parents, prior to their deaths, had deeded the ranch to Logan and Caroline, much of the business had already been established. So the couple worked rigorously to build their dream home—a three-bedroom, white wooden house with a wraparound porch. When that was finally finished, remodeling Logan's parents' old home to use for future ranch hands became their passion. When all of that had been completed, Logan and Caroline began to feel satisfied with their efforts toward improving the ranch and the success of their newly inherited cattle operation—so satisfied, in fact, that children abruptly became the top priority.

Caroline never thought she would have a hard time having a child. Coming from a family of nine, the idea just never crossed her mind. But after twelve long years of hoping and trying and praying, the couple was almost ready to give up completely. And, that was when a miracle occurred, and Luke made his debut into the Garrison family. However, because Caroline had such a hard time with her pregnancy, even through the labor and delivery, and because Logan worried until the very end about whether his dear Caroline would even make it through the childbirth, he vowed to himself that he would never again put her through that agony. So Luke had been their only child, the shining light in Logan and Caroline's eyes, and a constant joy to them as they watched him grow from an infant to a child and then into adulthood and this very special time, his graduation day.

By the time Luke pulled into the long dirt driveway back at home, the sun was up and most of the morning dew had disappeared. He could smell his mother's pancakes and sausage as he headed up the back steps into the house. "Something smells good," Luke said, hanging his suit on the back of the chair and checking to see if anyone had started breakfast without him.

"Come on in and wash up. Your food's getting cold just sitting here!" Caroline yelled from the pantry. "Your father should have been here by now. He left to check the cows on the other side of the creek a good half hour ago."

Luke replied, "I wish he would've waited on me. That ol' truck of his ain't strong enough to go plowing through that creek over there. He 'bout got stuck last week."

A little concerned, Caroline said, "Well, nobody said a word about it to me. Maybe you ought to go check on him—just for good measure, of course."

"Of course," Luke mumbled, heading out the door.

On his way to the truck, he heard the screen door slam from the ranch hand's house behind him. Luke gave a quick wave to Jim as he made his way to the truck. Jim hollered, "Where you going this time of the morning? You already finished with breakfast?"

"No, but Pa went to check on the cows this morning over on the other side of the creek in that dilapidated truck of his, and Mama and I were a little concerned."

"Here now, you go on back in that house and eat your vittles. I'll take care of your pa. He may be on up in age some, but he's smarter than a whip when it comes to taking care of himself and this ranch. He's probably just enjoying the scenery and taking his time. Don't you worry; I'll go hustle him up."

Luke thanked him as he walked back toward the house and the breakfast he had left behind. Jim had been with them for almost ten years now, and he was more like a part of the family than hired help. His tall, lanky build somehow disguised his enormous strength, and Logan had been pleasantly surprised when he first hired Jim. Overall, he was the epitome of a ranch hand, and the Garrisons knew how blessed they were to have him.

Luke ate hurriedly, wanting to get his chores completed before lunch so he could have the rest of the afternoon to enjoy himself before the graduation ceremony at six o'clock. As Luke headed to his room to change into his work clothes, he looked at himself in the mirror. People always said he looked just like his father, but for the life of him, he just couldn't see it. Not that he minded or anything. His father was a handsome man, standing at around six feet in height, with dark, wavy hair, brown eyes, and a muscular build that came from working on the ranch. He was tanned, of course, from being out in the sun, and his hands were callused and rough, but that had come from hard work and age. Luke, on the other hand, was six foot three, with the same jet-black hair and brown eyes, but with a youthfulness about him that had long since left his father. He too was tanned from the sun, and many people mistook him as being part Indian because of the deep color of his skin. He had a sharp, rugged look that seemed to be enhanced by the slight bit of stubble that hadn't been shaved since the day before. His good looks had always been a topic of conversation around school, but Luke never seemed to be aware of it, and even if he was, he never found the time or made known any desire to enter the dating scene like all the rest of his classmates. Eventually, most of the girls had given up hope of him ever finding them attractive.

When he heard sounds of a truck approaching the house, Luke hastily finished dressing and peered out the window. As soon as he saw Jim's face, he knew something had happened. He raced out of his bedroom and onto the porch, knowing before he spoke what the answer would be. "Where's Pa?" Luke asked, pleading for something other than the response he knew was coming.

"I'm sorry, Son. If I had gotten there just a few minutes sooner—the truck had turned over in the creek, and being as your pa couldn't swim—there was just nothing I could do."

Luke felt as though his breath was being sucked out of him as he slumped into the rocking chair. Caroline had heard enough through the screen door to know the outcome. She came out onto the porch and gently sat down beside

Luke. No one spoke, and there were no tears at first, mainly due to the shock of the situation. But after several minutes, when reality finally hit, the three of them couldn't stop the flow of tears, and they sat on the porch and wept.

The next few days were a blur of activity at the Garrison homestead. Neighbors from miles around dropped by to bring food and offer their condolences. Caroline and Luke spent a great deal of their time playing host to the guests; in fact, it seemed as though they were doing more consoling than they were being consoled. Graduation had gone on that Monday night without Luke and his family, and the black suit Luke had been so proud of had been pushed to the back of the coat closet by a well-meaning neighbor.

The funeral was held on Thursday, three days after the accident. It was a small outdoor memorial service held on the ranch, just like Logan had requested. Luke thought the irony of it all was that his father, years ago, had specifically asked to be buried in a small clearing by the creek—the same creek that would be the cause of his untimely death. As the close-knit group of family and friends huddled together following the close of the service, Luke couldn't help but blame himself a little. "If only I had come back sooner … if only I had waited until after breakfast to pick up my suit … if only I had driven him over to the other side of the ranch … if only…." All these thoughts kept running through his head until he was not only upset with himself but also angrier than he had ever been in his life.

For the first few weeks after the funeral, Caroline continued to weep openly every time the screen door slammed or the sound of a truck could be heard—or anything happened that remotely reminded her of her late husband. Luke, however, went about his chores with no emotion at all. All the neighbors were amazed at how well he seemed to be handling his father's death, but Caroline knew otherwise. She knew Logan's death had taken a toll on him, but she also understood that nothing would help Luke except time. There were days when Caroline thought she would go crazy. Not only was her husband gone, but in some strange way, a part of her son was missing, too—and there was no one in whom she could truly confide her feelings.

About a month after Logan's passing, Caroline was cooking breakfast in the kitchen. It was a day full of sunshine with no threat of rain—a great day for fishing. Normally, Luke would be rushing to complete his chores, eager to get an early start. But this morning there was no sign of Luke. Caroline hollered out the door at Jim, but no one had seen him since the night before. Suddenly concerned, Caroline headed for Luke's bedroom, where she found him sitting on his bed, lacing up his boots, with a half-packed suitcase beside him. "What are you doing, Son?" Caroline asked.

Slowly, Luke replied, "Mama, I've got to go away for a while. Pa's death has left me in disarray, and I can't seem to shake out of it. I know you always say that everything works out for the best, but I just can't find any good in this. I love you and this ranch and I know I'll be back to tend it, but right now, I can't even see what's next for me tomorrow, much less the rest of my life. Jim will take care of things until I get back. Please don't hate me or worry about me—I'll be fine. It's just something I gotta do."

As Luke spoke, Caroline stood there quietly, tears rolling down her face. Her light brown hair and ivory complexion had slowed the aging process somewhat, and people had often marveled at the fact that she had a son as old as she did. But looking at her now, Luke realized how much his mother had endured over the last month and wondered if she could survive without him. He knew this was something that had to be done, for his sake and the sake of the ranch. He just couldn't stand the thought of hurting his mother. Caroline sat down beside Luke, pulled him close to her, and gently said, "Son, I knew in my heart this day would come from the very moment you were born. A young person has to decide what to do with his life by himself—not by listening to others. Your pa and I raised you well, and I couldn't be more proud of you. You are everything I hoped you would be, and I know that whatever happens, you will do the right thing. But I do want you to think about something for me. If you're just leaving to sort through things, how 'bout considering a trip to your Uncle Charles and Aunt Louise's house in Shelby? They would love to have you, and it would still be far enough away that you could have some time to sort through what's bothering you."

Luke smiled a little. "Mama, you know me better than I know myself sometimes. I called Aunt Louise this morning. She's expecting to see me before nightfall."

"I knew you had a head on your shoulders. Take all the time you need. Jim and I can handle things here for a while. Just promise you'll call me from time to time and let me know how you're getting along. I don't want you going off and forgetting about me, now."

Luke grinned, "You act like I'll be gone for a year or more. I told Aunt Louise I'd probably stay for the summer. Jim needs me here at the ranch, and you do, too. I'll be back before the leaves start falling; you can mark my words, Mama."

Caroline leaned over and gently kissed Luke on the cheek. "Well, Son, you'd better come eat your breakfast and get on the road, then."

CHAPTER THREE

Shelby was a good four-hour drive from Bozeman, and by the time Luke had said his goodbyes and loaded up his things, it was already mid-morning. He was somewhat anxious as he made his way out of town. He planned to take his time and enjoy the drive, but the events of the past month had shocked him so much that he was beyond the point of enjoying anything.

As the sun shone straight down, proclaiming the noon hour, Luke began searching for a place to eat. A small, lonely diner at the base of a picturesque mountain seemed to be the answer to his hunger pains. Luke haphazardly parked his pickup between a '57 Chevy that seemed to be in decent shape and an older model Chrysler that may or may not have found its permanent home in that very spot in front of the diner.

As Luke claimed a corner booth in the empty restaurant, a haggard-looking waitress headed toward him with a greasy menu in her hand. "Hey, handsome. What can I getcha?"

Luke tipped his cowboy hat as a greeting. "Just a quick burger and iced tea, please. I'm not much for lollygagging around when I've got things to do."

The waitress nodded. Then with a quick smile and a flirtatious wink, she said sweetly, "Your order will be up in just a few minutes, and if you need something else—anything else—just holler. I'll be right over there, Honey."

Twenty minutes later was more like it as Luke finally sunk his teeth into his overcooked hamburger. Too frustrated to complain, he wolfed down as much as he could stand, then stood up to leave. "Check, please," he called out to the waitress, who had been staring at Luke since the moment he entered the diner. She slowly ran her fingers through her dingy blonde hair as she made her way down the aisle to him.

"It's so stuffy in here, handsome. How 'bout helping me wind down a bit since it's time for my break? I promise I can make it worth your while." She tried to nuzzle up against him, but he was walking out the door before she realized what had happened.

"Thanks for the invitation, ma'am, but like I said, I've got things to do. My money's on the table—just keep the change." And with that, Luke was out the door.

The rest of the trip was uneventful as the Ford truck wound its way up and over the Rockies. Then as Luke turned onto the dirt road that would eventually lead to his Uncle Charles's home, he was amazed as he observed a small herd of buffalo making their way across the open terrain. He pulled the truck to the edge of the road and sat for what seemed like hours, watching the herd. When they were finally out of sight, Luke pulled slowly back onto the road and headed to his destination.

As Luke had expected, Uncle Charles and Aunt Louise were watching for him on the porch of their ranch-style home. As his uncle helped him with his belongings, Luke could smell the freshly baked apple pie his aunt had ready for his arrival. Luke was shown to his bedroom, and after quickly unpacking, he headed back to the kitchen for a snack.

Uncle Charles and Aunt Louise had always been Luke's favorite next-of-kin on his father's side—Charles with his gold-streaked hair, hefty build, and a belly that seemed to increase a little bit each day, and Louise with her silvery-white hair, about as big around as she was tall. They were in their sixties, a little older than his own parents. However, like his folks, Charles and Louise tried for years to have a child. But they hadn't been as fortunate as Logan and Caroline, and the two of them never bore any children of their own. For years, they played host to several foster children, but that ended several years ago when Charles suffered a mild stroke. It had taken him more than a year to recover, and he still didn't do as much as he once had done. At least he was capable of performing his everyday chores, though, which was more than a lot of other stroke victims could boast. Nevertheless, the two of them were ecstatic about Luke's visit. It didn't take long for Luke to realize he had made the right decision as well.

Even though Charles and Louise had attended Logan's funeral, the trio still had a great deal to catch up on as they sat down at the kitchen table to enjoy their apple pie. Luke took the time to fill them in on everything that had happened back home on the ranch, while Charles told Luke a little about his own cattle business. Afterwards, Charles handed Luke a list of daily chores to complete. Louise had been reluctant for Charles to assign chores, but when Luke called them, he had been adamant about earning his keep, and Charles felt that he should honor the request. As Luke studied the list, he added, "Anything else you want me to help out with, I'll be more than happy to oblige. All you have to do is ask."

"You might not better offer too soon. Your Aunt Louise here might just take you up on that."

Grinning, Louise replied, "Oh, my mind's already a-turning! I do have a few rules here, though, that I am a stickler about, Luke. Breakfast is at 8:00 sharp, lunch is at 12:00 noon, and supper is at 6:00 sharp. Make sure you are washed and ready to eat—I don't like to have my meals getting cold because of a straggler. Also, you will be expected to go with us to church on Wednesday nights and on Sunday mornings. Other than that, what you do is your own business, as long as you stay clear of trouble, which I'm sure you will. If you need anything at all, just let us know. We're awful happy to have you here—it's been a long time coming."

Luke nodded, then picked up his dirty dishes and headed for the sink. As he reached for the door, he turned. "Like I said, if you need me to do anything else around here, I'll be more than happy to help. Just let me know. And I do appreciate your taking me in like this, especially on such short notice. It really means a lot to me—and to Mama." And with that, Luke headed outside to explore his new surroundings, the screen door slamming shut behind him.

"Man, that boy is having more of a time than I expected. It's a good thing he's here for the summer—maybe he can sort through the whole shebang before heading back home. I think I will take him up on his offer to add more work, though. Sure, I could use some more help around here, but more importantly, he needs to know as much about the cattle business as he can learn, because as soon as he gets home, the whole ranch will be on his shoulders."

Louise agreed. "Lord only knows the burdens he's carrying around right now. The sooner we get him settled in and busy, the better off he's gonna be."

The next morning after breakfast, Luke reluctantly joined his aunt and uncle in their pickup as they headed to church. The Garrison family had always been a church-going people, and Luke's parents were no different. In fact, as a child, Luke enjoyed the peaceful feelings he experienced whenever he attended. But over the years, he found himself beginning to daydream about other things, and eventually those feelings of serenity subsided. He found himself making excuses to his parents about too much homework or needing to finish his chores, and because they never questioned his antics, he got out of attending pretty easily. Since his father's recent death, he and his mother hadn't attended church at all. Caroline hadn't felt like going without Logan, but even more importantly, she knew how angry and resentful Luke was becoming, and she did not want to make matters worse. She could see that he didn't want anything whatsoever to do with church or the people who attended.

The little country church lay nestled all alone on a small hill just outside of town. Luke realized how beautiful it was the first moment he laid his eyes on it. The view was unbelievable—a rippling brook flowed gently to the side of the church, and the wildflowers were in full bloom all around it. The inside of the building was just as lovely, with its high ceiling and rich burgundy accents. It was small—probably holding a total of seventy-five people—but it was obviously worth the effort to attend, thought Luke, if only for the atmosphere. The service, however, was not quite as unique. The song leader led the group in several congregational songs before the preacher stood to deliver his message. Amazingly, Luke found himself actually listening to what the man had to say, and even though he would never have admitted it, he slowly began to relax—until out of the corner of his eye, he saw her.

Luke thought she was the most beautiful girl he had ever seen. In just a matter of seconds, he could feel a tingling sensation beginning at his feet and continuing upward, as if it would gradually consume his entire body. Gone was his attentiveness to the preacher—not that he cared at all. He consciously searched her up and down, taking note of her every detail. She had long, naturally curly brown hair that fell perfectly down her back. Her olive complexion indicated little makeup and was intensified by the small row of freckles left on her nose by the sun's rays. She looked to be about five foot seven, if not taller. She wore a long black dress that fell almost to her ankles and black shoes to match—and Luke couldn't take his eyes off of her. He was so captivated by her that Charles had to punch him as the congregation stood and bowed for the closing prayer.

When the benediction was over and Luke opened his eyes, the girl was gone. He swung around to look for her but caught only a glimpse of her hair as she pulled the door shut behind her. Then, with everyone eager to stop and meet him on his way out of church, Luke didn't have time to look for her again. But she was the only thing he thought about as he graciously nodded and shook each stranger's hand.

When they arrived home, Charles, Louise, and Luke headed for the kitchen to finish off the leftovers from the night before. Louise had made sure Luke realized that, in order to get to church on Sundays, little time was allowed for cooking, and leftovers were the norm for their Sunday dinners. Luke could have cared less what was on the menu today, though, as he found himself thinking only of the girl from church and fantasizing about what she was doing.

He thought briefly about asking his aunt and uncle about her, but he decided not to mention anything just yet. After dinner was over and the dishes were cleared from the table, Luke headed to his room to rest. He tossed and turned as he tried to sleep, but his mind continually ran away with him with thoughts of the girl. He could hardly wait until Wednesday night church services, and he vigorously prayed that she would be there again.

CHAPTER FOUR

T**HE FIRST OF THE WEEK WAS NOT EXACTLY** eventful for Luke as he spent his time helping out on the ranch. Charles had taken Luke up on his offer to help, and extra job duties were added each day. Luke didn't mind, though, because even though he had been around ranching all of his life, his uncle went about doing things differently than his father had, and Luke found that the more he worked, the less he felt angry about the events of the last month. Plus, although Luke already knew a good bit about cattle, his father had always taken care of the more difficult duties, and Luke quickly found himself learning more about ranching than he had ever thought possible. By suppertime each night, Luke was worn completely out. After the dishes were done, he would excuse himself to call his mother and then would head to his room for the night. Louise worried about him not spending more time with them in the evenings, but she refused to pressure him at this point. Instead, she prayed that eventually, Luke would warm up to Charles and her, and that he would trust them enough to confide his feelings in them.

Luke, however, didn't dwell too much on the past, but instead was anxious about the church service on Wednesday. He spent hours daydreaming about the girl he'd seen and couldn't help imagining what their next meeting would be like. When Wednesday finally did come, he was so nervous that after dinner, he dropped his plate, and pieces of it scattered all over the floor. He apologized profusely, but Charles and Louise were more worried about Luke than they were about the inexpensive dish. When all the pieces were gathered and thrown away, Luke excused himself and headed outside to calm down before it was time to leave for church.

The fifteen minute drive couldn't have been any longer for Luke as he twisted and turned and tried to find a comfortable position. No one spoke, which left Luke to indulge in his own thoughts. As soon as the truck came to a halt in front of the church, Luke's eyes began searching for the mystery girl; but unfortunately, she was nowhere to be found. When the congregation stood to sing the first song, Luke began to realize the girl was probably not going to show up. He knew how crazy it was to think something could happen between them—first of all, he knew absolutely nothing about her, and secondly, he had no experience in the area of romance. But for the life of him, he couldn't get her out of his mind.

As the preacher stood to begin his sermon, the door creaked, and Luke assumed someone had stepped out for a moment, as people sometimes did. He wasn't even planning to look, as his mother had always considered that to be rude, but he couldn't deny himself one last chance to search for the girl. And as he turned, there she was—even more beautiful than the first time he had seen her. She wore a casual denim dress and sandals, her hair pulled back and away from her face.

Luke had to make himself turn back towards the preacher, but even after that, he never heard a word the man said. He was too busy practicing what he would say to her—because this time, he had promised himself he would meet her, even if he had to burst through the crowd and introduce himself. And that's exactly what happened.

Several families were in attendance that night that hadn't been able to meet Luke the previous Sunday. Trying not to be rude, Luke pretended not to hear his aunt and uncle calling his name as the service ended and people began dispersing. He quickly pushed his way out into the aisle and headed for the door. When he finally made it outside, he could see the girl turning the corner. He sped up in order to catch her and, when she finally noticed him, she stopped. "Were you needing to speak to me about something?"

Luke's knees almost gave out at the gentle sound of her voice. "Uh, no, I just, well, I'm new here and I was just, um, trying to meet everyone. I saw you Sunday, but you left before I had an opportunity to introduce myself, so—hi, I'm Luke Garrison."

She replied, in a somewhat reserved manner, "Nice to meet you, Luke. I'm Emily—Emily Alderman. I'm in somewhat of a rush, so maybe I'll see you around."

Stunned at her quick departure, Luke said, "Well, wait, what's your hurry?"

"I just have something I need to tend to, that's all," she said as she turned around and headed toward a beat-up Chevy truck that looked more rust-colored than the navy blue it once was.

Luke tried to think of something to say—anything to make Emily stay a little longer. But all he could think of was, "Will I see you Sunday?"

Emily, already pulling away from the church, called out, "I try to take one day at a time, Luke—anything after that is usually beyond my immediate control." And with that, the truck sputtered as it pulled onto the gravel road.

Luke stood and watched until the truck was out of sight, then slowly turned around—right into the path of his Aunt Louise. "Where have you been? There are several people waiting to meet you—why in the world did you run off?" Without waiting for a response, she grabbed him by the arm and said, "Oh, never mind, just come on—you've got to socialize to fit in around here."

More introductions were made, followed by a brief stop at the preacher's house for dessert and coffee, but Luke didn't mind at all. He was on cloud nine—greeting everyone, adding to the conversations, and laughing along with the crowd, but only thinking of Emily and counting down the days until he could see her again. He was pleasantly surprised, however, when a chance meeting between the two of them occurred much earlier than he had expected.

CHAPTER FIVE

Loud thunder and rain beating on the roof woke Luke earlier than usual that Friday morning. *Good,* Luke thought, *I can sleep a little later this morning!* But being used to early rising, Luke couldn't for the life of him fall back asleep, so he decided to get dressed and maybe help Aunt Louise with breakfast. Luke found his aunt rolling out the dough for homemade biscuits. Even though he offered several times to help, she refused to let him. So Luke just sat and watched, making small conversation as his aunt worked away.

About the time the biscuits were ready to pull from the oven, his Uncle Charles came into the kitchen. "Luke, today we'll head into town. There are some supplies we've been needing, and your aunt needs some groceries. We can't do much around here anyway with this rain, so we'll make a morning of it."

This excited Luke—a day off during the week was scarce, if not unheard of, and he was tickled to be going into downtown Shelby for the first time since he'd arrived. He was full of questions for both his aunt and uncle all through breakfast, and the couple was excited that Luke was enjoying himself for once.

As the truck made its way into town, Luke tried to imagine what the little town of Shelby would be like. He figured it would be a lot smaller than Bozeman, but that wasn't a problem to him. He was still interested in seeing the sights. And besides, to Luke, anything was better than working—at least today, anyway. About ten minutes went by before the truck made it into the city limits. The rain had slacked up quite a bit by that time, and Luke glanced to see his aunt putting aside the umbrella she had so desperately searched for prior to leaving the farmhouse. He chuckled to himself and thought, *That's just like a woman.*

Once they dropped Louise off at the entrance of the grocery store, Luke and Charles headed to the mercantile to get the supplies they needed. They spent a few minutes milling around the place but never once saw anyone claiming to be an employee. Just as Charles was beginning to get a little irritated, Luke turned to find himself face-to-face with Emily. Although she was in blue jeans and an oversized flannel shirt, Luke believed she had to be more beautiful than he had remembered. A huge grin lit up his face, but he tried to maintain a somewhat casual demeanor as he said, "So, you work here, do you?"

Emily looked as if she had no idea who Luke was. She smiled cautiously and replied, "Yes, this is my uncle's store. Do you know him?"

Luke, realizing that she was actually unsure of who he was, answered, "You obviously don't remember me. I met you at church Wednesday and talked to you for a minute after the services. I'm visiting here for the summer."

A sense of recognition showed on her face, and she replied, "Oh, yes, I'm sorry. I see so many people here in the store that sometimes I forget names and faces. I apologize."

Luke smiled, "No harm done. I'm Luke. I've been staying with my Aunt Louise and Uncle Charles for the last week. I'm not usually too good with names, either—but yours I remember. It's Emily, right?"

Emily blushed. "You're right. I'm Emily. Can I help you with anything today? We have a few things on sale over in the corner."

Luke caught the hint in Emily's tone of voice that today was going to be business only, so he motioned for his uncle to come over with the list of supplies. Luke stood back and watched as Emily took the list and with great ease collected the items his uncle requested. He couldn't help but notice her figure as she worked to find the items they needed. Within a few minutes, all the supplies were gathered together at the front register of the store. Luke hated the fact that the shopping took such little time, but he realized that he was just a stranger to Emily—and besides, she probably had a boyfriend anyway. *Who am I kidding?* he thought. *Someone as beautiful as Emily can have anyone she wants. I'm a fool for thinking otherwise.*

But just as Luke was about to leave, he saw something that made him question whether his initial impressions that day were right. His uncle had already walked out with some of the supplies, but because Luke had been so much into his thoughts, he had dropped his sack of supplies all over the floor and was scurrying around, trying to gather up all the items. As he searched for the last can, he felt Emily's presence behind him and turned to meet her warm gaze. She bent down, reached her hand over, took Luke's hand in hers, and gently led it to the lost can. Without saying a word, Emily stood, smiled a sweet smile, and said very softly, "Have a good day, Luke."

Luke felt as if he would never have to breathe again. Just having Emily touch him caused his emotions to run wild. He began to think he had been dreaming when he heard his uncle holler from the doorway, "Luke, are you going to stay there on the floor all day, or are you going to come on home with me?" Luke stood and turned to see that Emily was now gone, and nothing was left of the moment the two of them had shared except his emotions and the can he held tightly in his hand.

Louise's grocery shopping turned into an entire morning of errand running. When Charles and Luke finally caught up with her after their mercantile experience, Louise had not even made it to the grocery store yet. Although Luke was somewhat irritated, Charles was used to these mutual trips to town. And when Louise left the two men and headed into the next little shop filled with inexpensive trinkets, Charles informed Luke that his wife would be at least another hour or two. "I'm going to take a stroll down to the pharmacy and catch up on this week's news. Wanna come?" he asked. Luke thought about it but decided to explore the quaint little town of Shelby by himself. So he said goodbye to his uncle and headed across the street in the opposite direction from which they had come.

Luke's first stop was a bait and tackle shop. He had forgotten how much he loved to fish until he entered the store and began milling around a bit. Working with his Uncle Charles had really kept him on his toes lately, and Luke hadn't really had time to think, much less fish. He maneuvered through the aisles of fishing rods, bait, tackle boxes, and the like, taking his time and breathing in the odors of the place. He vowed to make it a priority to go fishing at least once a week from now on, no matter what was happening around the farm. Somehow he doubted his aunt and uncle would mind.

"Can I help you with something, sir?" the clerk asked.

Luke turned to see a silver-haired man standing in the doorway. *He can't be taller than five feet,* Luke thought to himself. The man wore rather large bifocals that covered most of his face, and the little bit of stubble around his cheeks and chin proved he couldn't have made a beard even if he had tried. He was dressed in his fishing gear, complete with fishing hat and boots, as if he himself was heading to the lake for a good time. "Uh, no sir, I was just looking," Luke said aloud.

"Are you looking for anything in particular?" the man asked Luke.

"No, sir, I'm really just wasting time—my aunt is shopping, and my uncle is at the pharmacy. I'm just wandering around, basically."

"Oh, you're Charles and Louise's nephew," the man said as he reached to shake Luke's hand. "Yep, sure was sorry to hear about your pa. From what I remember of him, he was a fine man indeed. I'm John—John Crawford. I own this here place, yep. Not much to it, but it puts food on the table. I own the mercantile, too."

So, this is Emily's uncle, thought Luke. *Things are getting better all the time.*

Luke grinned and said he had already made a trip to the mercantile today. "I didn't see you there, though."

"No, my niece usually handles that place for me, as much as she can. Yep, I try to help her out all I can. Oh, but that's another story. Listen, I came over from the pharmacy. If you need anything, just holler at me over there. I trust ya, Son."

"Sure, no problem, Mr. Crawford. Thank you, sir."

As Mr. Crawford headed back across the street, Luke chuckled to himself—the fact that these men gathered at the pharmacy to gossip like a bunch of women was hilarious. After thinking about it, he almost headed right after the man, just to see what was so interesting in that place. But he decided against it and figured he might just need to look around in the mercantile one more time, just in case he had forgotten something the first time he had been there.

Luke tried to calm his heart from beating too rapidly as he made his way once again to the mercantile. He was petrified everyone he passed would be able to see his flannel shirt rising and falling at a ridiculous rate of speed. But he wanted to see Emily—and if he had to embarrass himself to do it, then so be it.

Everything was quiet as he entered the store, and no one was at the counter. "She must be in the back again," Luke said to himself. But five minutes passed—and still no Emily. Luke wondered if she just hadn't heard him milling around in the store. He purposefully picked up a book and dropped it on the floor, hoping to get some attention, but no one came. After another couple of minutes roaming around the store, he decided to head out to find his uncle. *I'll have another chance to see her,* he thought, *maybe even sooner than Sunday, if I'm lucky.*

As Luke left the store, Emily slowly came out from her hiding place. She had seen Luke coming and had hidden behind the counter until he was gone. She knew it was stupid, and her back was killing her from hunching over for so long, but she knew it was better this way. She didn't need anyone, especially a man, coming into her life right now. She had too many problems to deal with, and it would just complicate things that much more. Besides, Luke wouldn't want to be around her anyway if he knew the secrets she kept. It just wasn't worth it, she told herself, and she vowed to avoid him from now on—no matter what.

CHAPTER SIX

WHEN SUNDAY CAME AROUND AGAIN, LUKE WAS UP and dressed before his aunt and uncle were even stirring. In fact, he had taken care of most of the morning chores and was getting out the ingredients to make pancakes when his aunt came into the kitchen. "Well, land sakes, Luke, I must have overslept a little. I'm so sorry—have I absolutely starved you, dear?"

Luke smiled sheepishly and said, "No, Aunt Louise, I just couldn't sleep this morning. I hate that I woke you. I mean, it's only seven. I'll cook breakfast this morning—you deserve a break." But Aunt Louise would hear nothing of it. She grabbed her apron and before wrapping it around herself, used it to swat Luke out of the kitchen.

Luke decided to sit on the porch and enjoy what was left of the sunrise. Mornings in Montana were like a little piece of heaven, and watching the golden rays slowly light up the ranch made it hard for anyone to experience it without a few breathless moments here and there. He wondered what Emily was doing at that very moment. He imagined she was probably still asleep. "I bet she's even more beautiful when she's asleep," Luke thought aloud.

"What'cha talking about, Luke?" Uncle Charles asked through the screen door.

"Oh, nothing, Uncle Charles. Just thinking out loud."

"Well, how 'bout thinking aloud as you're eating your breakfast?"

"Sure thing, Unc," Luke said as he headed into the kitchen and the abundant breakfast awaiting him.

Aunt Louise was an excellent cook, but on Sunday mornings, she always outdid herself. Since Sunday dinner consisted of Saturday evening leftovers, Aunt Louise had extra time to devote to a full breakfast on Sunday morning.

This Sunday was no different as Luke sat down to pancakes, ham, bacon, eggs, and homemade biscuits. He surprised himself with the amount he consumed, but he knew Aunt Louise was thrilled. Cooking was her greatest passion, and when someone turned one of her dishes down or disliked the taste of it, she took it personally.

Finally, after a third helping of pancakes—and after working to win an argument with Aunt Louise about the fact that he was, indeed, too full to eat another bite—Luke excused himself to do his chores and get dressed for church. His aunt and uncle could hear him whistling as he headed toward the barn. "I believe our boy is beginning to settle in around here, Louise. Must be that fine cooking of yours," Charles said with a sly grin.

"Oh, Charles, you'd think my cooking was good even if I burnt every last bit of it," Louise laughed.

"Well, burned or not, there's no doubt I got the best-looking cook around." And with that, Charles stole a quick kiss before going out the door to help Luke with the rest of the morning chores. Once those were taken care of, Luke and his uncle had just enough time to shower and shave before Aunt Louise was hustling them out the door for church.

"Sure looks like a huge turnout today," Luke commented as the threesome pulled up at the little country church. "I'd have never guessed this many people ever showed up considering the congregations I've seen so far."

"Yea, well, everybody shows when it's eating time!" grimaced Aunt Louise and, for the first time, Luke noticed the pots of food his aunt had in the floorboard of the truck. Luke realized what all that messing around in the kitchen last night had been for.

"What are you talking about, Aunt Louise?" he asked.

"Oh, I thought I told you—today's the fifth Sunday of the month, so we have dinner on the ground after the church service. It's something we've always done. That's why all the people show up—they keep track of fifth Sundays, kinda like Easter and Christmas. People just come out of the woodwork."

And Aunt Louise was right. As the Garrisons made their way toward the church steps, more families were arriving in everything from rundown farm trucks to shiny new four-door sedans. Some were dressed in the finest clothes Luke had ever seen—women in tailored suits with matching hats, and men in suits as well, some even in three-piece suits. Those dressed in such finery, Luke noticed, were the very ones with no children and no food.

No wonder Aunt Louise is resentful, Luke thought. *These people have more money than any of us, but instead of pitching in and helping with the food, they just show up to eat what all of us bring. It's not like they're here because they haven't had enough food on their own table or anything.*

Luke noticed that Aunt Louise wasn't the only one frustrated with the fifth Sunday crowd. The church was obviously divided—the regulars on one side, furious that someone else was inhabiting their weekly pews, and the fifth Sunday visitors on the other side, irritated by the lack of respect they were receiving. Luke and his aunt and uncle found a seat on the very back row, which suited Luke fine, but aggravated his aunt to no end. However, once the service began, everyone seemed to settle down a little bit, and the preacher's sermon seemed to be uplifting to them all. In fact, Luke decided then and there that this preacher was pretty smart indeed—instead of delivering a fiery sermon on judging others or coveting your neighbor (which is what everyone deserved), the wise elder spoke only of God's love for His people. And as the closing prayer was spoken and the congregation dismissed, slowly the two very different crowds merged together.

It was then that Luke caught the first glimpse of Emily making her way through the crowd of people. *Man, I got so caught up in the church members' attitudes, I totally forgot to look for her at all,* Luke thought, angry at himself for going even a minute without the beautiful image of Emily weighing on his mind. As Luke's eyes continued to follow Emily through the crowd, he realized he was going to miss any chance of talking to her, for she had already worked herself past the group of people and was headed straight for her truck. But then Luke saw something rather odd. Emily's uncle, Mr. Crawford, made it to her before she closed the truck door and began to talk. As Luke watched, the conversation between the two became somewhat heated, and eventually Emily said something to her uncle, jumped out of the truck, slammed the door, and headed straight back to join the congregation for dinner. After watching her march off, Mr. Crawford spun around, headed to his truck, and drove off in a hurry.

By the time Emily had approached the group of ladies preparing the tables of food, she had a smile on her face and showed no sign of what had just transpired a few moments prior. In fact, no one was the wiser—except Luke, who had no idea what had happened between Emily and her uncle but knew it must have been major for Emily to become that upset and change her plans altogether because of it.

"Hey, there," Luke said casually as he passed Emily in line. She was standing on one side of the table, helping serve food. Luke was on the other, filling his plate as fast as he could. Somewhat cautiously, Emily smiled, acknowledging the greeting but offering no reply. "Are you by yourself today or with someone?"

"By myself," came her reply.

"Good, then you can eat with us," a voice from behind them called. Luke and Emily looked at each other, then turned to see who had spoken. It was Aunt Louise. Luke looked perplexed, but Aunt Louise just pushed him on through the line. "Get all you want, but keep the line moving. We women still have to eat, you know." Luke kept moving, thinking how strange Aunt Louise's bold remark to Emily had been—but grateful for it just the same. Although Aunt Louise hadn't actually been in line behind Luke (it was still the custom there for the men to eat first, followed by the women and children), she had somehow been close enough to overhear the conversation, Luke guessed. Why else would she have invited Emily?

But Luke was wrong. Aunt Louise had just acted on the instinct that had been burdening her for days. Unbeknownst to Charles, Louise had been studying Luke. She had noticed the way his attitude changed last Sunday after church. At first, she thought Luke had heard something in the sermon that brought back a little peace in his life, but then she realized he was acting as if he were in love. And according to Aunt Louise, it didn't take a surgeon to figure it out—just a woman with a little bit of intuition. As Louise watched Emily take her plate over to the blanket where Luke and Charles were eating, she felt a surge of excitement. "I truly hope Luke and Emily at least become friends. It would be good for them both. She's so shy and confined within herself—she needs to forget the past and go on," she surmised. "And Luke—well, he needs someone to help him believe in life and love and—well, all the good things life has to offer." She quickly grabbed her plate and headed over to the blanket, anxious to see what she could do to jumpstart the relationship budding between Luke and Emily.

CHAPTER SEVEN

EMILY SURVIVED DINNER ON THE GROUND SIMPLY BY answering each question Aunt Louise addressed to her. She answered them politely but without any additional details. So while Emily felt as though Aunt Louise was grilling her for information, Aunt Louise was actually struggling to keep the conversation flowing, and in her own mind, just trying to be polite. In contrast, as much as the two women worked at it, Luke and Charles did nothing to help matters. The two men sat in silence, oblivious to the peril each woman faced.

Finally, as dinner ended and the ladies of the church began cleaning up, Louise stood up and announced, "Emily, I'll handle the cleanup while you and Luke take the food I brought to the truck for me." Obediently, Luke and Emily headed to the tables to find Aunt Louise's food. As if in a trance, Luke covered the four pots and pans and handed two of them to Emily. They walked in silence to the truck. Luke felt his mouth suddenly go dry as he worked up his nerve to speak. A weak "thanks" was all that came out, but Emily quickly responded with a "you're welcome," and the conversation had finally begun.

Before they knew it, the twosome had walked away from the vehicles and over to the tree that held a cozy swing for two. Not knowing what else to do, Emily took a seat and motioned for Luke to sit as well. They pushed the swing with their feet until it was easily moving back and forth. Luke began, "Have you always lived in Shelby?"

"Oh, no, I moved here about three years ago."

"Really—where did you move from?"

"Oh, I've lived in several places, but I guess you could say I'm a Georgia peach originally—at least, that's where I was born."

Luke was intrigued. "Wow, I guess that's the reason for the slight accent, huh? I've never even visited outside of Montana, much less lived anywhere else. What's Georgia like?"

Emily sighed. "Well, I can't say I remember much—we moved from there when I was ten. But, from what I do remember, it's a flat state compared to here. Most people will tell you there are actually two Georgias—southern Georgia is full of rural towns and lots of farmland; the northern section contains most of the larger cities and the majority of the state's population. We southerners always felt looked down upon in a way—most families worked in the fields, growing cotton, peanuts, corn, and tobacco, while those in the northern parts worked in banks and held office jobs. Even though my dad was a salesman, there was a major difference because of where he was from. And even though I was small, it was pretty evident, even to us little ones. Anyway, my hometown is a place called Ocilla, named for a famous Indian chief—Osceola, I believe. Actually, a number of my relatives still live in Ocilla."

Emily stopped, stared off into space, and seemed consumed in her memories. Luke, on the other hand, was fascinated. Emily seemed so quiet, but as soon as she began discussing her childhood and Ocilla, she immediately offered details and even became somewhat animated as she spoke. "Have you been back since you left?" Luke asked.

"To Ocilla? Oh, no—we moved to Oklahoma from Ocilla when I was ten. We've moved since then, obviously, but I've never gone back to Georgia, although I'd like to someday."

"May I ask why you moved?"

Emily became still, then quietly commented, "You know, after you move several times, the reasoning behind all of them tends to run together. Which makes me wonder—what made you move to Shelby, Luke?"

Luke slowed the swing to a stop and took a long breath. "Well, first of all, I'm only visiting for the summer. See, my dad died last month unexpectedly, and, well, I just needed some time away—to sort things out, I guess you could say."

Intuitively, Emily reached out and gently touched Luke's hand. "I'm so sorry—you and your dad must've been pretty close, huh?"

Luke turned away, trying to hide the sudden brightness of his cheeks and the slightest hint of moisture in his eyes. "Yeah, I guess you could say that.

Plus, I'm an only child, too, if that makes any difference. Do you have any brothers or sisters?"

Suddenly feeling a little too close for comfort, Emily ignored Luke's question and slid off the swing. Turning to Luke, she said, "I really hate to go, but I have a lot to get done this afternoon. Thanks for the company."

Luke jumped from the swing and grabbed Emily's arm as she turned to walk away. "Hey, wait, is that it? When will I see you again? I mean, I thought we were making some good conversation just then. I've even talked to you about my pa, and I haven't done that with anyone. Don't just walk away."

Emily could tell Luke was, in a sense, pleading with her—not only to stay, but also to commit to more discussions in the future. She had promised herself she would avoid him, but Aunt Louise had given her little choice. *Then again*, Emily thought, *this whole thing's Uncle John's fault. Oh, he absolutely infuriates me at times. If it hadn't been for him, I wouldn't have had to eat lunch with Luke or talk with him, and I certainly wouldn't have opened up to him like I did.*

"Emily, are you listening to me? Did you hear a word I said?"

Shaking her head as if coming out of a trance, Emily asked, "What?"

"I said, didn't you hear me?"

"Look, Luke, I told you before that I live one day at a time—believe me when I say it's really all I can handle. Some days, I don't even think I can do that. I appreciate our talk today, but I'll just have to see you when I see you. That's all I can give, and I'm asking you to understand."

Luke, although unsatisfied, gave a weak smile. "I guess I'll have to. Emily, I'm here if you ever need to talk. I'd really like it if we could be friends." Emily nodded, then turned and headed to her truck.

As Luke made his way back to the remaining congregation, he saw Emily pulling out onto the road that would take her home. Despite her abrupt departure, Luke couldn't help but smile. Emily was not only beautiful, but sweet and smart—and yes, mysterious. He knew without a doubt that he and Emily were meant to get to know each other better. The big question in Luke's mind, however, was how could he convince Emily of this?

CHAPTER EIGHT

As Emily drove away from the churchyard, she was furious with herself. In fact, the more she thought about her conversation with Luke Garrison, the angrier she became. She had decided to avoid Luke at any cost, and she had failed. Even if Uncle John had made her go back to eat, she should have kept her own mouth shut. "Oh, but no, I had to just flap it until I almost said too much. I'm so stupid—stupid, stupid, stupid," Emily decided minutes later as she pulled up to the run-down, four-room shack she referred to as her burrow. Outside, the house was surrounded by junk. Old, rusted tire rims, used farm equipment, and other useless items leaned against the wooden exterior and decorated the yard, which was, to say the very least, in desperate need of mowing. Emily looked around in disgust as she sidestepped several empty cans to make it to the door.

The inside of the house was shabby but clean. Emily tried her best with what little money she made to keep her living quarters livable. Although she spent a lot of time at her uncle's store, at home she concentrated on making things as bearable as possible. Emily headed through the kitchen into the bedroom she called her own. She changed from her Sunday dress into jeans and a flannel shirt and pulled her hair back into a working bun. Then she quietly knocked on the other bedroom door, opening it gently. The figure lying in bed looked small as Emily leaned over to adjust the covers. Slowly, the figure turned in her direction. As if in a childlike state, the face focused on Emily, gave a weak smile, but said nothing. Emily forced herself to smile back, smoothed the hair away from the face, and fought back tears as she returned the gaze of what was left of her mother.

CHAPTER NINE

Luke's luck for seeing Emily seemed to run out after the fifth Sunday dinner as a new work week began and sunshine became ever-present on the ranch. It seemed that all of a sudden, Luke and his uncle were so swamped with work that Aunt Louise made not only the weekly trip to town alone, but also the Wednesday night and Sunday morning church services as well—all for different reasons and circumstances.

The trip to town was actually no big deal—Uncle Charles had already told Luke that Aunt Louise sometimes went alone to town. But the trips to church—well, unusual work circumstances prevented the men from attending both times, although that certainly didn't help Luke's feelings at all. He was, to say the very least, extremely disappointed at the idea of Emily being there and him not.

As for Wednesday, the day started out busy, but the plans still were to quit work in time for supper and a quick shower before church. In fact, Uncle Charles was heading back across the pasture to check on Luke when he saw one of his cows in trouble. She was lying on the ground with four or five other cows standing over her as if they were concerned for her well-being. Charles pulled the truck over a short distance from them and slowly made his way toward the herd. As he got closer, the cows parted to let him through to the one in pain. Once he was by her side, he knew exactly what the problem was—the cow was giving birth, and the unborn calf was turned wrong. Unless he got help and the calf was turned by hand, both the calf and its mama would soon die. With little time to spare, Charles headed out to find Luke. He would definitely need his help for this.

Luke was working to finish a fence at the end of the pasture when he heard the sounds of his uncle's truck. As he looked up, he realized his uncle was shouting something. Luke began walking toward the truck when he finally made out enough of the words to realize a mama cow was in trouble. He swung the door open and hopped in, ready to help in any way he could.

As the truck maneuvered through the pasture and back to the herd, Charles filled Luke in on the situation at hand. The two of them figured they had less than an hour before the cow and her calf would be beyond saving. It was crucial to get the calf turned and birthed as soon as possible.

When they arrived, Luke immediately donned a pair of gloves from the back of the truck while Charles lassoed the cow and secured her to a nearby tree. Luke positioned himself along with Charles at the cow's rear, and the two grabbed hold of the baby calf's feet, which were already protruding out of its mother. It was all the two men could do to keep holding onto the calf to turn her. Finally, when Luke thought all hope was gone, the calf began to turn enough to pull it out of its mother. With all the strength they could muster, Luke and Charles grounded themselves and pulled the calf out. The mama cow groaned in sheer agony. Immediately, the rope was loosened, and the healthy newborn calf was laid beside its mother.

Charles hollered out, "Luke, you birthed that calf as good as I've ever seen!"

"Yeah, I've had lots of practice—Pa always made me handle this kind of thing at home. He said it was quite a blessing to be involved in an actual miracle."

"Well, he was right—kinda makes you stand back in awe of God's creations."

"Yeah, I guess so—although I'll never understand some things, like who is He to decide when to take my pa? And why now?"

It was the first time Luke had opened up to Charles, and it took them both by surprise. Charles touched Luke's shoulder and said, "Whether you believe it now or not, Son, God's timing is always perfect, and He never makes a mistake. Right now, I know it's hard, but in time, maybe you'll come to more of an understanding of it all." Luke didn't comment as they finished up with the cow and calf and climbed into the truck to head home.

Louise was just walking out the door for church when she caught sight of the two men. She hollered, "I'll be late if I don't go on now. I left your supper on the stove. I'll clean up when I get back." Charles mumbled a "thank you" as he headed in to wash up. He was glad Louise had always been understanding when work got in the way of church. It was rare, but when something did happen, Louise took it in stride and did her best to make Charles know she supported him in what he did.

Luke waited on the porch, watching Aunt Louise drive off until he couldn't see the taillights any longer. He hated that he would miss the opportunity to see Emily again, but it was no one's fault. He knew from growing up on a ranch that work sometimes took precedence over other things, including church. Regrettably, those situations always seemed to occur at the most inopportune times. "At least I'll see her again Sunday—I guess I can wait that long," decided Luke as he headed in the house to the supper Aunt Louise had left for him.   Unfortunately, Luke was wrong, for when Sunday came, another catastrophe hindered the men from attending the worship service. The morning began like any other Sunday morning—chores were started before breakfast so that the only thing left to do afterwards would be to ride through the pasture to feed and check the cows. Normally this took about an hour, giving the men just enough time to get back to the house and shower before Aunt Louise started fretting. She hated to be late for anything and would begin fussing a good fifteen minutes before it really became necessary, just to drive the point home and still get there on time. Nevertheless, this particular Sunday left Luke wondering if he would ever see his mystery girl again.

As the two men rode through the pasture, they noticed the number of cattle was low. At first Charles assumed some were in the woods off to the other side of the creek. But upon closer inspection, he realized something was dreadfully wrong. He figured at least seventy-five cows were unaccounted for, so he and Luke got out of the truck to begin looking around for tracks, worried some type of wild animal had gotten through the fence and killed them.

"But there aren't any dead cows lying around, Uncle Charles. Don't you think there'd be tracks if it were bears or something?" Luke asked.

Agitated, Charles growled, "You got any better ideas?"

Luke ignored the question, focusing his attention instead on a section of the woods that didn't look quite right to him. As he made his way over, he noticed a path had been made through the weeds and brush – a path that wasn't supposed to be there. He called to his uncle to follow him as he continued on, his heart pounding as he became more and more anxious about what he would find.

"There couldn't be any of them hurt because they'd be bunched up in a group, wouldn't they, Uncle Charles?" Luke asked.

When he got no response, Luke tried again. "Wouldn't they be crowded together if one of 'em was hurt?"

Again, no response from Charles.

Just as Luke was getting ready to ask for a third time, Charles tensed up his lips and said, "Son, to be successful here, we can't take time to dawdle. One thing's for sure—something's wrong, and time is of the essence. Stop talking, look around for clues, listen for any sounds, and let's try to get to the bottom of all of this."

As Luke began walking away from his uncle, he stopped and turned back to say a quick "yes, sir," when Charles decided to drive the point home with the boy. "Don't even think about wasting time to acknowledge what I've just said, Boy. Following orders is the best way to show you know what to do—not by using that mouth of yours."

Luke tightened his jaw, shook his head, and headed farther down the path to a section of the pasture he knew quite well.

If anything's happened in this part of the woods, I'll be the first to know it, he thought to himself.

Luke began meandering his way through the trees and brush, and as he did, he began to notice tracks in the mud—not just a couple, but quite a lot of tracks. He continued his search, his heart sinking a little lower into his stomach with each step. As he came to the end of his uncle's land, Luke felt a sickening feeling envelop him, and he became faint. For there in front of him stood what was left of the fence his Uncle Charles had sent him to repair the week before.

Luke was devastated. Not only had he been totally thrilled that his uncle had given him a task to complete on his own, but before today, he would have put his fence-building skills up against anyone's. He had worked on fences for years with his father, and besides the occasional small repairs needed here and there, nothing catastrophic had ever happened to his fences. All of a sudden, his expertise was no more. He had spent three entire afternoons mending that fence, and now he realized it had taken less than a week for it to be destroyed. He had caused problems for his uncle, and Luke knew Charles would be disappointed. He felt like a total failure.

"Oh, God, what will Uncle Charles say?" Luke cried out.

"Uncle Charles is gonna say get that chip off your shoulder and get down there to that fence and examine it. Find out for sure if your repair work caused this before any blame is cast."

Luke's shoulders tightened as he spun around to see his uncle standing there with jaws clenched and eyes dark, determined to know the truth. Luke slowly bent over towards the fence, scared to see what the truth really was. With shaking hands, he began to examine the remains of the barbed wire. A puzzled expression was followed suddenly by a sigh of relief as Luke realized that the real truth was—it wasn't his fault after all.

"Uncle Charles, come look!"

Charles knelt beside Luke, and taking the wire into his own hands, said, "Well, I'll be. This here's what you call sabotage, plain and simple."

The wires had been cut and the fence destroyed on purpose.

"But who would do such a thing—and why?" Luke asked.

Charles stood up, eyes ablaze, and answered him through clenched teeth. "This land of mine neighbors another ranch owned by a man named Jack Hawkins. Hawkins is about as hardhearted a man as you can find. Oh, he's been successful and has money and all, but there ain't a bit of ethics nowhere in him. He'll lie, cheat, and steal with the best of 'em, and when you see him coming, you know trouble's sure to follow."

"Has he always been like this?"

"No, Son, that's the sad part of it. A long time ago, Jack and I were good friends. Seems like another lifetime, to be honest with you. We were big buddies in grade school, but we had our hearts set on the same girl—your Aunt Louise. Actually, I had my heart set on her, and he had his mind set. I honestly don't know if the man has a real heart. Anyway, Jack promised your aunt the moon and stars and everything else, but she chose her love for me instead. Although the two of us have done really well, it was mighty tough at first. I guess that's why I love her so much. She could have had everything money could buy—but she chose me."

"Wow, so Mr. Hawkins has had it out for you ever since?"

"Well, after Louise and I got hitched, Jack found someone else. He seemed to have gotten over all that had happened between us, and we became friendly again, to a small degree. But something happened between the two of them—no one really knows what—and Jack became bitter all over again, to everything and everybody, but especially to me. The past twenty years, anything he could do to cause me pain, he's done it. When the hundred acres between my ranch and his became available four years ago, I was given first dibs because old man Gentry left it like that in his will. But Jack went behind my back to the Gentry children and offered double, so the land became his. I wasn't surprised, because that's just how he operates."

"So what's happened since he bought the land?"

"Oh, nothing major. He fought landlines for a while, but the deeds were clear. I hadn't seen or heard from him again until the other day when we made the trip to town. He was at the pharmacy getting a prescription filled when I walked in. Usually, when I see him or he's out and about in town again, trouble's a-brewing. I knew it would be just a matter of time before I heard from him again."

"Can't you file charges or something for this?"

"I suppose I could, but I won't. See, I promised your aunt a long time ago that I'd try to always turn the other cheek when it came to Jack. She still believes there's good hidden somewhere in that old dodger. One day, he may do something to me that's too terrible to ignore, but right now, as long as I can recover most of my cows and have this fence repaired, little if any permanent damage has been done this time."

Uncle Charles took one last look at the fence and began the short trek back to his truck. "Come on, Son, we need to get some more wire from the barn before any more cows get out."

Luke, somewhat perplexed at what his uncle just said, trotted after him. "So, let me get this straight—you're not mad at him? You're just going to go on and forget about all of this? How can you do that?"

Charles leaned against the front of the truck and explained, "Son, I never said I wasn't mad. Hell, I'm mad as fire. But, I'd rather get over it and go on about my business than to go back on a promise I made to your aunt. She's what matters the most to me. And another thing while we're on the subject—life's not simple, Son. There are no guarantees, and life's not fair. All of life's experiences—from having to deal with an enemy all your life to having to deal with the death of a parent—are difficult. They can make you bitter, or you can become a better person because of them. And it's always your choice. But I'll tell you, my experiences prove to me that life is more rewarding when you work to become the better man."

He tipped his hat to Luke and chortled, "And that's your sermon for the day! I won't even collect offering from you!"

Luke snickered. "It's a good thing—you'd owe me money for having to listen to all that!"

Charles took his hat off and popped Luke over the head, and the two were still laughing as they pulled back up to the house.

CHAPTER TEN

B<small>Y THE TIME THE TWO MEN HAD FINISHED</small> eating their normal Sunday dinner of leftovers and Charles had taken the time to fill Louise in on what had transpired that morning, it was past time to get started on the mending of the fence. Charles had been wrong when he said he thought he had enough wire in the barn. So he'd sent Luke into town for some more, while he himself climbed on his tractor and headed over to the Hawkins' ranch in search of his missing cows.

Although Luke only needed to stop at the Farmer's Supply for the wire he needed, he considered for just a minute running into the mercantile to see if Emily might be there, but he decided against it. Because his day had been filled with work, Luke had actually forgotten it was Sunday. So he was quite surprised when he pulled up to the supply store and the door was locked. Luckily, the sign on the door told Luke that he could go around to the house out back and knock if it was an emergency. Of course, that also made Luke remember it was indeed Sunday and that a quick stop at the mercantile would obviously have done him no good anyway, since it would be closed as well.

Luke headed toward the little white house located behind the supply store, knocked a couple of times on the wooden screened door, and waited for an answer. He watched as an elderly woman slowly made her way to the front of the house. Luke called out, "Hello!" to her, but she didn't reply.

As she got closer, she lifted her head, smiled, and asked, "Hello, Sonny. What brings you here this afternoon?"

"Ma'am, I'm awful sorry to bother you, but I need some wire from the supply store, and the sign said to come back here if it was urgent—and, well ma'am, this is pretty urgent."

"Well, I wish I could help, but Frank left just a little bit ago for the Alderman place. Lord only knows when he'll be back from there."

"The Alderman place—is that by chance Emily Alderman's family you're talking about?"

"Yep, it's one and the same. Poor souls—there ain't nothing else can happen to them worse than what's already been. But, I ain't one to talk about things—I just pray for 'em."

Luke shifted nervously. "Emily's okay, isn't she? I mean, she's not sick or anything, is she?"

"I suppose she's as best as can be expected, considering all she's been through. But like I said, I ain't one to talk about things such as that. You know, Sonny, Frank leaves an extra key to the store somewhere. If I can find it, you can get what you need and just leave a note for Frank. I'm sure your uncle has an account."

Surprised, Luke asked, "How do you know who I am? Have we met already? You know, I've met so many people, I'm not too good at remembering everyone."

The old woman laughed, "No, Sonny. We haven't met. But I do know who you are. You're Charles's nephew. One thing you'll learn real quick here—word gets around, especially when a stranger comes to town. Just typical talk in town, nothing personal. Of course, I'm not one to talk, but I do listen quite well. No, I don't get to church nowadays—just can't hold out anymore. But I do still get the news, you can be sure of that."

She pushed open the screened door and motioned for Luke to help her down the front porch steps.

"Come on, and I'll look for that key. Nope, Frank won't mind a bit if we put your supplies on Charles's account."

The two of them made their way to the back entrance of the store, and shortly thereafter, the lady had found the hidden key and Luke was able to find the wire he needed to repair the damage to the fence.

"I really appreciate you going to all this trouble for me, but I better get going. Uncle Charles will wonder where in the world I'm at."

"Oh, it's been no trouble at all, Sonny. Your visit has certainly been the highlight of my otherwise uneventful day. You come back anytime."

As Luke loaded the wire on the truck, he realized he hadn't even asked for the lady's name. "You know, ma'am, I didn't even catch your name. I apologize—how rude of me."

She smiled. "No, Sonny, I didn't really offer it. My name is Evelyn Cartwright. My son Frank owns the store. He and his wife took me in when my husband passed on last year. You've probably seen them at church. Elaine is the organist—has been for years."

"Oh, yes, I remember seeing them—they are part of the regulars."

Evelyn laughed aloud. "Yes, they are. I see your aunt has filled you in on some things. That Louise—she's quite a character. Fine, fine family, the two of them are. You are blessed, young man, don't you ever forget that or take it for granted."

"Yes, ma'am, I am very thankful for Uncle Charles and Aunt Louise. They've been good to me." And helping her up the steps to the house, Luke thanked her. "Mrs. Cartwright, it was definitely my pleasure meeting you, and I hope to see you again real soon. Thanks again for all your help."

"Any time, Son, any time." And Mrs. Cartwright headed back into the house.

By late Sunday afternoon, the majority of the damage to the fence had been repaired, thanks to the extra wire Luke had gotten. Charles had even had some luck of his own while Luke was gone. He'd been able to single handedly retrieve over thirty of his cows from the Hawkins' ranch. Then as he was leaving, he had a brief encounter with Hawkins himself. And whatever was said between the two of them ended in the remaining cattle being returned to the Garrison ranch first thing Monday morning. Luke was surprised that it ended the way it did, without much of an altercation, but Charles reiterated the fact that this was definitely not the last time they would have to deal with Jack Hawkins.

CHAPTER ELEVEN

By the end of the next week, almost two weeks had passed since Luke had seen Emily. The irritation of not being able to see the girl of his dreams coupled with what Mrs. Cartwright had said about everything Emily had been through and was still going through had Luke in a state of worry. And if that wasn't enough, Luke had spoken to his mother the night before, and she had indicated to him that the last few days for her had been rough, which made him concerned that he'd made the wrong decision when he left her alone for the summer.

Gradually this worry turned into bottled-up frustration, and suddenly this frustration turned into a total lack of patience for everything and everyone. The Luke who Uncle Charles and Aunt Louise had been so happy to get to know was now hidden behind a mask of anger and aggression. The smallest things set Luke off so much that by Saturday night, Aunt Louise felt as if she had to tiptoe around him with everything she did. And nothing was ever right anymore. If that wasn't enough, rain and thunderstorms settled in and awakened the already edgy family to a rather dismal Sunday.

Charles came in from the morning chores soaked from head to toe and mad as a hornet. Luke had slept in and didn't help with the chores at all. Breakfast came and went—and still no Luke. Neither Charles nor Louise wanted to deal with a confrontation before church, so Luke's actions were ignored. The two of them dressed for church and headed out without a word. Once inside the truck, though, Charles let out a huge "Humph," slammed his hand on the steering wheel, looked over at Louise, and said, "You know what? I've had just about enough of his shenanigans. Just because he feels like crap doesn't mean that it's okay to treat us like that. We've opened up our home to this boy and catered to his every whim. If he's going to act like this after all we've done for him, I'd just assume he acts like that at home. We're a little early leaving today, so I think I'll take a minute to get all of this off my chest once and for all."

Louise silently nodded, scared to utter a word. She could count on one hand the times Charles had lost his temper, and she never cared to see him in this mood. But she knew it was something that Charles had to do as well as something Luke deserved to hear.

By the time Charles made it to Luke's bedroom door, his temper was raging. He threw the door open to find Luke sitting on his bed, staring out the window, still in his pajamas. He never moved as Charles entered the room, nor did he acknowledge his uncle's presence. "Listen here, Boy, I've had about enough of you and that attitude of yours. After all we've done for you, have you no gratitude? Your snarly remarks and outbursts this week—well, I can handle them, but your aunt Louise? Well, she neither deserves to hear them nor deserves to be anywhere near anyone who acts in such a devilish fashion. She's done nothing but love and care for you, and you treat her no better than a sack of potatoes—something that's a burden to deal with, to say the least. I'm sick of it, and I'll tell you what, if you can't act any better than this—well then, you've just worn out your welcome. You can pack up them there bags of yours and take yourself back home to your mama. I know you've been through a rough time, but it's time to suck it up and move on. If you can't do that and come to terms with what's happened, then you're not the Luke we thought you were anyway. You might as well go on home to your mama so she can waste all her energy on babying you. She doesn't have your dad to pamper anymore, so it might as well be you she spends her time on."

Luke's head slowly turned. "Don't you ever talk about my pa like that again. He loved my mama and she loved him."

"Let me tell you something, Boy. You think you're all grown up, but you can't even hear what I'm trying to say. That thick skull of yours won't absorb anything it doesn't want to. You keep on and you'll turn out to be nothing like what your pa and ma wanted you to be. What a blessing you'll be to them then."

A quick lunge by Luke and a sharp left hook startled Charles, and he cried out as the pain registered and he slid down against the door frame. He reached up to feel fresh blood running down from the side of his lip. "What the—" Charles began as Luke slowly backed away, horrified at what he'd just done.

"Oh my God," Luke muttered as he slumped back on the bed.

Charles got to his knees, grabbed hold of the door frame, and steadied himself in order to pull himself upright. He reached into his back pocket and took out his handkerchief to stop the blood flow. He could hear Luke softly sobbing behind him as he turned and gradually made his way out of the bedroom, but he had nothing else to say to him. As he headed out the front door to join Louise in the truck, he had the sinking feeling that Luke would be gone by the time the two of them returned.

Louise was devastated when she saw Charles and then learned, on the way to church, what had unfolded during his and Luke's brief encounter.

"How could this happen?" she kept repeating. "Where did I go wrong?"

"Honey, as much as you love him, he's not ours. He's only been here for part of a summer, and he brought a whole load of problems with him when he came. The boy's got to want our help before we can help him. It's a two-way street—you can't do all of it."

"I know, but it doesn't help my feelings about it. Charles, he's got so much going for him, but all of a sudden, he can't seem to see that. And I thought he was making so much progress. But now it's like he's got blinders over his eyes. And, well—it just breaks my heart."

"Like I said, Louise, the boy's gotta want our help. Otherwise our efforts are useless. It's out of our hands now, anyway. Luke will be gone by the time we get back home."

"Oh, no," Aunt Louise began to sob. "Turn around, Charles. Turn around, I say. We've got to talk some sense into him—please, Charles, turn around."

Tenderly, Charles laid his hand over Louise's. "No, darlin', I won't turn around. I can't. It's not the right thing for us to do—and it's not going to help matters at this point. It's Luke's call now, not ours."

Louise looked at Charles as tears fell from her eyes. "I know you're right, but it doesn't make me feel any better. Sighing, she added, "I guess we really need the comfort of church today, huh?"

She began to pat her face dry with her handkerchief in order to make herself a little more presentable. Out of the corner of her eye, she could see Charles dabbing his lip and chin and then she realized that there would be no covering up the situation. Charles's lip had already begun to swell, and his lower face was turning purple as it began to bruise. *Oh, well,* she thought as the truck pulled to a stop and the two of them headed inside, hand in hand, hearts heavy. *If anyone can help us through this, it's the Lord and our church family. Might as well quit trying to pretend.*

CHAPTER TWELVE

Uncle Charles was only partially right in his predictions, for Luke wasn't home when he and Louise got home from church. Still, he wasn't on his way home to his mama, either. Instead, Luke had made a decision, and he was on a mission.

As Luke sat on his bed, trying to calm down, he found that all the pent-up anger and resentment he'd felt since his father's death had finally come to a head. He cried uncontrollably for more than an hour, and when all the tears were gone, he felt empty and hollow. All the extra baggage he'd been carrying with him was no more, and all that was left was a feeling of nothingness. Luke didn't know what to think or how to feel. He took a few minutes to pack his bags, sure that Charles and Louise expected him gone when they returned. With a few extra minutes left before church would be over, Luke took a quick shower to revive himself a bit. Heading out, he lingered only a moment at the front of the ranch house before closing the door behind him. At that moment, he had no idea if he'd ever return to his aunt and uncle's home. He knew he was responsible for what had gone wrong between the three of them, and a deep guilt enveloped him—but at the same time, he was extremely grateful for all the love and support he had received from them throughout his brief stay.

Even as he pulled out of the driveway, Luke was unsure of where he was going. He knew going home to his mother wouldn't solve anything. *She definitely doesn't need me to deal with right now,* Luke thought to himself. At the end of the driveway, he instinctively turned toward town. A few minutes later, he realized what needed to be done. He pulled the truck to a stop in front of the supply store he'd visited the Sunday before. He walked right past the entrance to the store and made his way to the little white house behind it. He never flinched as the lady he knew as Mrs. Cartwright made her way to the front door.

"Well, now, what have we here? Why, Luke, what a surprise to see you again—and so soon. The store's actually going to be open this afternoon—they're planning to take inventory if you need something."

Luke gave her a weak smile. "Oh, no ma'am—actually, I came to see you. I need some help, and I think you are just the person who can help me. I mean, if you don't mind. I don't want to be a burden by no means."

"Oh, Sonny, come on in and have a glass of lemonade with me. If you only knew how little I'm needed nowadays, you'd understand how thrilled I am to be of help to you."

The two made small talk as Mrs. Cartwright poured two glasses of freshly squeezed lemonade and set them in front of Luke.

"If you're not in a big hurry, dinner will be ready in about an hour. Elaine likes to practice her organ pieces after Sunday services, so we usually eat around 1:00. Won't you stay?"

"Oh, no ma'am. I really don't have time. In fact, let me just get down to it. You mentioned the Alderman place last Sunday when we talked, and I'd really appreciate it if you'd tell me how to get there."

Mrs. Cartwright looked perplexed. "Now, what on earth do you need to go over there for?"

"Mrs. Cartwright, please, I really don't want to get into all of it right now. I just have something needing to be taken care of, and I have to go there to get it done. Will you please help me out here? I'm sort of in a bind."

Clearing her throat, Mrs. Cartwright answered, "It must be awful important to you. I guess you have your reasons for asking—but, you know, Luke, your aunt and uncle know where the Alderman place is, too. But, I guess you have your reasons for not going to them with this as well. No matter. I'll tell you how to get there. Just keep in mind—they aren't ones for company, usually."

"I'll keep that in mind, ma'am."

Once Luke had the information he needed, he headed over to the sink with his empty glass and again thanked Mrs. Cartwright for her help. "Thanks again for your hospitality." He squeezed her hand as he passed by her, and headed to the door. "Don't get up—I can let myself out."

"Good luck, Luke, dear. I hope you find the answers you're looking for."

The sun was blazing as Luke headed back to his truck. The town of Shelby was deserted except for the occasional car passing by on its way home from church. Luke headed through town, turning on a little dirt road about three miles out. The road split a half mile down into two separate lanes. Choosing the one to the right, Luke slowed to a crawl as the trees and brush became thicker and the road narrower. Finally, Luke noticed a small clearing. It was then that he saw the run-down Alderman shack—totally forsaken, by the looks of it. He was somewhat taken aback by it, but humbled just the same. Had it not been for the fact that Luke knew the truck Emily drove, he never would have believed Emily lived in such conditions.

He let the truck idle for a moment as he took a few deep breaths. He knew what he had come for and what he needed to do, but that didn't make it any easier for him. As if his courage might waiver if he waited any longer, Luke took one last breath, yanked the door open, jumped out of the truck, and trotted to the front steps. He felt like he was running an obstacle course as he sidestepped the clutter in the yard. Gaining some momentum, Luke took the front steps two by two and was just getting ready to knock on the screen door when it swung open to reveal an irritated and somewhat embarrassed Emily. Looking around as if there may be others with Luke, she grimaced. "What do you want? Why did you come here?"

Luke was stunned. "Ah, well, ah—I just needed to see you, Emily."

"Why, Luke? You barely know me. What could you possibly want from me that's so urgent it calls for a visit?"

"Ah, well, I just … I mean, I just needed someone to talk to and, I guess, well, I thought we'd become friends."

Eyes ablaze, Emily countered, "Oh, you thought, huh? That was mistake number one. You know what? You thought wrong. How dare you barge onto my property without my permission? Who do you think you are? You know what? I don't even want to know. Just go. Get out of here. Go, I said!"

Bewildered, Luke began backing up as Emily demanded him to leave. Taking one step too many, Luke's foot slipped. He tried to grab the railing on the porch, but he couldn't get to it quickly enough to keep himself from falling flat on the ground. Much to Emily's dismay, she didn't have time to react, either. All she could do was watch as Luke fell.

Emily ran to Luke's side. "Oh, oh—are you all right? Luke, are you hurt?"

"Yeah, I'm fine—just stupid."

"No, it's my fault. Are you sure you're okay?"

"I said I'm fine," Luke bellowed. He swallowed and then spoke less aggressively. "Just give me a minute. Then I'll leave you alone."

Emily moved away from him, giving him the space he needed. He took a couple of deep breaths and pulled himself up. A sharp pain shot through his ankle, making his knee buckle and causing him to fall back down on the dirt.

"Oh my gosh, you are hurt. Luke, where does it hurt—your knee, your ankle, where?" Emily cried.

Luke scowled. "Oh, so now you're my friend? Look, Emily, I can handle myself. No need to concern yourself. It's probably just a sprained ankle."

Emily began to soften. "Luke, please. You're hurt. Let me at least help you back up on the porch so we can take a look at it. I'll get some ice for you so maybe it won't swell too badly."

She reached out her hand, and Luke took it. The two of them made their way to the steps, and Luke sat down on the top step.

"I'll go get that ice—why don't you take your boot off? I'll be right back."

Frowning, Luke ever so slowly pulled off his boot and then leaned back against the porch rail and closed his eyes. Emily was back in a minute and helped Luke put ice on his ankle. The two were silent for a while, not knowing what to say.

Finally, Luke couldn't take it any more. "Emily, I'm sorry. I should never have come here. I just wanted to see you and talk to you. I haven't seen you in a couple of weeks, and I thought we had made a connection before. Some things have happened to me in the last week or so and I thought they would somehow make more sense if I talked it all over with you. I'm really sorry."

Emily sighed. "Of course, I would have much rather seen you somewhere else. I'm not used to letting people see where I live, Luke. It's not anything I'm proud of and, well, I'm just used to being left to myself. I've gotten kind of fond of living that way, actually."

"Yeah? Well, to be on your own this young, making a living, I mean, I know you want more. We all do. But I think you're making a good start. But then, that's just me, and I don't know a lot about anything.'"

Emily turned away from him. "No, you don't know anything about this. I mean, you don't know anything about me at all—where I come from, where I've been, or even what secrets I hide."

Surprisingly, Luke chuckled. "Oh, good grief. Everyone has secrets, Emily. I have my own skeletons in the closet that I don't care to share with anyone else. But that doesn't stop me from making friends, and it shouldn't stop you, either."

He reached over and touched Emily's hand. "If you have secrets, that only means you're human. And if the secrets belong to you, I'm sure they're the sweetest secrets ever."

She blushed and pulled her hand away. "I believe you came to confide in me, not me in you."

Luke sat up straight and took on a serious look. "Yeah, I guess you're right. The truth is—I moved out of my uncle and aunt's house this morning. They don't particularly want me there anymore, and I can't necessarily blame them. I most definitely can't go home. I've just screwed up everything lately, and I don't really know how to fix what's happened."

"All right, all right, slow down, and tell me everything that's happened. I mean, until I know the whole story, I have no idea what you're talking about.'

"Sorry. I guess I really should start from the beginning, huh?"

CHAPTER THIRTEEN

For most of the afternoon, Emily sat by Luke as he bore his heart and soul to her. He described in detail the day his father died, how it nearly killed his mother, and how he decided right then and there to never let his feelings show. He explained his decision to come to his aunt and uncle's house for the summer, and how meeting Emily had been the best thing to happen to him in a long time. He ended by telling her about the feelings he'd dealt with over the last couple of weeks—the anger, the frustration, the confusion—and how he'd chosen to deal with it only when everything exploded and he had no other choice.

When Luke finished, he sighed and turned to see Emily wiping tears from her eyes. He was surprised that what he'd said had made such an impact on her. Emily shrugged. "Luke, I'm sorry you've had such a tough summer. I wish there was something I could do to help."

Luke reached over and touched her shoulder. "Oh, but you have, Emily. Don't you see? You've done more for me than anyone else has in the last few months. You listened. I haven't felt comfortable enough to talk to anyone about this until now. You have no idea how grateful I am. I just wish I could undo what has happened. I mean, I know I can't get my pa back, but I'd sure like to be given another chance to react to it. I sure screwed it all up the first time around."

"So you've made some mistakes—who hasn't? It doesn't mean you can't make amends. You've heard of second chances, haven't you?"

He shook his head. "Yeah, I suppose I have. I've just spent so much time being angry at God and everyone else. I don't know how to go about correcting that kind of thing."

"Well, you can start by saying you're sorry. Luke, I don't believe in coincidence. I believe all things happen for a reason, even if some are beyond our control—like your pa's death. But I also believe you choose how you react to the circumstances you find yourself in. You may not have but one shot at some things...." Emily trailed off for a moment. Swallowing hard, she continued, looking Luke straight in the eyes. "Luke, you have the opportunity to correct these mistakes. Please jump at the chance." Turning away, she added under her breath, "Some people would give their whole existence to be able to change the past."

Not hearing Emily's last comment, Luke glanced down at his watch and exclaimed, "Gracious me. Look at the time. I've been talking so much, I completely forgot about lunch. You must be starved."

"Actually, no, I had a quick bite before you showed up."

"Oh, good, I'm glad to know...." Luke stopped talking the instant he heard the noise coming from inside the house. "What was that?" he asked.

"What was what?" Emily acted as if she hadn't heard a thing. But then Luke noticed that she had taken on a new sense of urgency. "Well, I'm glad you feel better after our chat. And I'm sure your ankle will be just fine in a couple of days. Why don't you start working on mending things with your aunt and uncle, and I'll be sure to check with you at church next week to see how you're getting along." She turned and grabbed the screen door about the time another noise was heard inside. This time Emily couldn't keep herself from flinching. Luke was certain that this time she had heard the same thing he had.

"Emily, what is that noise? Is there someone in your house?"

The screen door slammed, and Emily whirled around to face Luke. "You know, you chose to come here and confide in me. I sat and listened and acted like a friend to you—against my better judgment, I might add. But that doesn't give you the right to meddle in my personal life. My business is my business, and I'd prefer to keep it that way. I do pretty well handling things without anyone to confide in. Now if you don't mind, you have some apologies to make—and, well, I have responsibilities of my own."

Desperate to prolong their visit, Luke grabbed her arm. "But Emily, I can be here for you if you need me—just like you've been here for me...."

Another sound came from inside. Emily pulled away from Luke and again pulled the screen door open. "Didn't you hear a word I said? I don't need you to be here for me—in fact, I don't need anyone. Just go. Social hour is over." With that, she quickly slipped into the house, leaving Luke standing there flabbergasted at what had just taken place.

CHAPTER FOURTEEN

Although Luke hated the way things had ended that afternoon with Emily, he did act on her advice. He knew she was right about making amends for how he'd acted and what he'd done. So he left Emily's and headed back where he'd started from.

Charles and Louise were sitting on the front porch rocking as Luke sauntered up the walkway. He could tell by their expressions they were not only surprised to see him but at the same time, somewhat relieved to know he was all right. Charles stood up and began, "Luke, Son, I …"

But Luke would allow no such compromise. "No, Uncle Charles, I believe what I have to say needs to be heard first, if you don't mind." He noticed that his uncle's lip was swollen and the lower part of his cheek bruised. But that just added fuel to his fire as he continued. "First, I want to say how grateful I am for the two of you taking me in the way you did. I know you've gone out of your way for me, and whether you believe it or not, I do appreciate all you've done. Second, I know that everything that went wrong here between the three of us is totally my fault. Neither of you has done anything to provoke the behavior you've had to witness from me. And you certainly didn't deserve to be on the receiving end of my foolish behavior. Uncle Charles, I'm so very sorry for striking out at you. I probably don't deserve to be forgiven for the way I've treated you, but I am truly sorry."

Aunt Louise pulled a tissue out of the pocket of the housecoat she sported on Sunday afternoons. Dabbing her eyes, she started to speak, but again Luke stopped her. "Wait just one more minute, please, Aunt Louise. I need to get all this off my chest before I lose my nerve. When Pa died, I saw how it nearly ripped Mama apart. I felt like I needed to be the man of the ranch, so I vowed never to show my emotions—to keep everything inside so that people would see that I was capable of taking over for my pa and that I was responsible and mature. I thought hiding your feelings was the manly thing to do. But I didn't realize that not allowing yourself to deal with things has huge consequences. And that certainly proved true as I became more angry and confused and irritated—at no one in particular—but since you both were here, I took it all out on you. I have spent most of today finally allowing myself to deal with the feelings and emotions that have been haunting me the last couple of months. I can't say that I don't hurt anymore, but I sure feel a lot less heavy and pent up inside. I hope this is the beginning of the healing process. Again, I apologize. I would love to spend the rest of the summer with you, but I totally understand if you would rather I not."

He stood there, waiting for a reply, but got nothing. Charles and Louise stared at Luke and then each other for what seemed like an eternity. Finally, Louise burst out crying and headed straight for Luke. "Oh, Luke, we love you so much. We're just so worried about you. Of course you can stay with us. We'd be honored to have you." As Luke and Louise hugged, Luke cut his eyes over at his uncle.

Charles looked stern. "Luke, I agree with your aunt. I think you ought to stay the rest of the summer, but I have a couple of conditions in order for you to do that."

"Charles!" Louise exclaimed. "The boy just apologized to you—what else do you want? Can't you see he's sincere?"

"Oh, I have no doubt about that," Charles replied. "I just want to be certain that, from now on, things continue to improve. I'd hate to have something like this happen again."

Luke nodded. "I agree. What do I need to do to make amends?"

"Oh, this isn't to make amends, Luke. You've done that. Apology accepted. But, I have two new rules you must follow to continue your stay here. Number one, from now on, if something is bothering you or if you need to talk about your feelings, you must confide in us. Otherwise this living arrangement will never work. You've been going to your room and spending time there after supper when we feel it would work better if you'd spend that time with us in the living room."

"Sounds good to me," Luke agreed. "What else?"

"Well, number two is this—don't ever use that fist on me or anyone else in this household again. No negotiation on this one."

"It's a deal!" Luke grinned sheepishly as he reached out and hugged Charles. He found himself thinking of Emily, as it was her idea to try and make things right. But as Louise led him into the kitchen for a mid-afternoon dinner, he told himself that he'd have to think about Emily later, when he was alone in his room and could go back to everything that had taken place at the Alderman home earlier that afternoon. He had lots of questions to go over about their encounter—why she didn't want him there, why her attitude changed when Luke fell, what the noise was that he heard inside the house, and why she changed again to cover it all up. He'd think about all of that later, he told himself.

It was bad enough having to put that part of the day off, but to make things worse, Aunt Louise was back to her old self, asking questions and trying to get Luke to open up to her. He knew that, eventually, word would get out that he'd gone to see Emily at the Alderman house, especially since he'd had to ask Mrs. Cartwright for directions. But he decided that until he could sort through all of his questions on his own, he would keep that tidbit of information to himself for a little while longer. He hoped it wouldn't cause problems down the road for him, but he just couldn't talk about any of it until he had it clear in his mind what had actually happened. *I'll tell Aunt Louise more about it in a few days, at least before she has time to get to town or to church again. That way she'll still hear it from me instead of the Shelby communication line,* he thought, and then chuckled under his breath. *These small towns—they are definitely something else.*

CHAPTER FIFTEEN

When Luke awoke Monday morning, he felt good. He'd lain awake in bed the night before, going over and over in his mind the conversations he and Emily had shared. Although he still couldn't understand her erratic behavior, he believed he knew the cause of it. Emily was hiding something—and not just from him. "There must be something she doesn't want anyone to know," Luke mused. "Whatever it is, it must be pretty terrible for her to withdraw herself from everyone."

"Luke! Breakfast!"

Luke hurried to finish lacing his boots. Aunt Louise was right about meals being served at a particular time. He'd never seen a woman's fury like Aunt Louise's when his Uncle Charles would be a few minutes late for one reason or another. Cooking was her pride and joy, and she expected all participants to be on time with stomachs empty and appetites raging. Luke was particularly good at living up to the task.

"How'd you sleep, Son?"

"Good, thanks. Mmmm, hotcakes and sausage—my favorite!"

"Well, help yourself. There's plenty. Charles had to get moving a little early this morning, so it's just me and you."

As Luke devoured his first helping of pancakes, Aunt Louise laughed, "Whoa, slow down, dear. There's plenty where those came from—relax and enjoy them. They go down better when you take time to chew 'em."

Luke grinned. "You know, you're a right sassy thing when you want to be."

Louise winked. "Gotta keep Charles on his toes a bit."

The two of them enjoyed a laugh as Luke piled his plate with a second helping. They continued the light-hearted meal until Charles came in to get Luke for morning chores. And even after that, Luke's day went well. He felt better, he seemed more relaxed around his aunt and uncle, and he had seen Emily. He even found time to call and check on his mother, and to his surprise, she also sounded much better than she had when they'd last spoken. All in all, things finally seemed to be looking up.

On Tuesday morning, Luke awoke to a heavy downpour, and he was thrilled. He was hopeful that this meant a trip into town for food and supplies, which would also mean a stop at the mercantile. But he was disappointed when he found out this wouldn't be the case. He tried not to let it get him down, though. Amazingly, it didn't, because at lunch, Aunt Louise informed him of something so terrific that the news seemed to make his whole week. As he and Charles entered the house and began washing up, Luke noticed several pies and cakes sitting on the counter. "Land sakes, Aunt Louise, you planning to feed an army?"

Louise's eyes lit up. "Actually, I'm getting ready for tomorrow night's Fourth of July celebration downtown."

"What celebration?"

"Oh my, I thought we'd told you. It's one of the biggest events of the year, if not the biggest!"

"Well, what is it exactly? What do you do?"

"Son, it's like this," Uncle Charles started. "The women bake days in advance to see who's the best cook in town, although everyone knows it's my Louise. She's won that contest every year."

"Oh, Charles." Louise blushed.

"It's the truth. Ask any of the men in town."

"Why not the women?" Luke asked.

"Son, here's a lesson you should learn and never forget. Never question a woman's cookin'. You ask any of the womenfolk around about this cooking contest and who's won, and they all get real defensive."

"Oh, so you just tell me my cooking's the best to shut me up, do ya?" Louise started at Charles, rolling up her dishrag and aiming it at him.

"Of course not. You are definitely the best cook around. I'm just giving my nephew a lesson about all other women!" He grinned as Louise threw the dishrag at him. He grabbed her in a bear hug and planted a big kiss on her cheek.

Luke laughed. "Okay, okay, so we know what the women do. What else about this festival?"

Charles continued. "Oh, you just can't get the full effect of it till you've experienced it yourself. There are cooking contests, foods galore, game booths, carnival rides for the kids, bingo—you name it, we got it. All the stores close at noon, and the town is transformed into something right out of the movies. Everything is set up on Main Street, and everyone from miles around shows up mid-afternoon with lots of food and hearty appetites. The food is spread out on tables, and people just help themselves throughout the night. At eight, there's a dance under the pavilion with a local band and everything. Then at nine, the fireworks start. And if I do say so myself, the show gets bigger and better every year."

As Charles went through all the details of the celebration, Luke began to feel like a kid again at Christmastime. He couldn't wait for the carnival, and he knew in his heart of hearts that Emily would be there. He wanted to know as much about the festival as he could. He asked Charles how the festival was paid for and what profit came from it. Louise answered, "This isn't a fundraiser, dear. It's a celebration. No one gets a dime—it's just all volunteers, even the band. And to finance it, each volunteer covers their own expenses. 'Course, the actual booths were built a few years ago by some of the men. We just use them over and over again each year. Some volunteer to do booths, and they supply the prizes for them. It's a community event, you see."

"Who thought of it, and when did it start? Have you always done it?"

Charles explained, "Well, about eight years ago, we were going through some tough times, sure 'nough. It hadn't rained in months, and people were really suffering on their ranches and farms. A lady by the name of Mrs. Cartwright...."

"You mean Evelyn Cartwright?"

Louise joined in. "Why, yes. How do you know Evelyn? She hasn't been to church in months."

Luke thought a minute before answering. "Let's see. I met her that Sunday I had to go to town for some wire. The store wasn't open, and I had to ask her to help me out. Then I went back again to see her this past Sunday."

Louise looked puzzled. "Hmm, that's odd. She didn't say a word to me about it. And, I just spoke with her...."

"Anyway," Charles interrupted, "Mrs. Cartwright had been to a celebration such as this several years back when visiting her sister down in Oklahoma.

The women's auxiliary had been discussing ways to boost the morale of the church members when she brought up the idea to have a celebration here. The ladies loved the idea, and it just went from there."

"Did it help?"

"Did it help what?"

"Did it help the feelings of the church members?"

"Oh, you can't imagine the change we saw in some of them. From cross and cranky and 'woe is me' to lending a hand to others in more dire circumstances. It literally changed the mood of the entire town. It was amazing. And so, ever since, there's never been a question about whether we'd have another one. It's a given."

"What do you contribute, Uncle Charles? I mean, I know Aunt Louise takes care of a good bit of the food."

Louise beamed. "Charles finances the fireworks show each year."

Proudly, Charles added, "Yep, my boy, you're looking at the one financial backer for that shindig. Lots of hard-earned dollars go into that show, and it's all worth it. It's definitely the highlight of the night."

"What can I do to help, then? I want to do something."

"Oh, there's no need, dear. Charles and I donate plenty."

"I know, and I don't mean to be difficult, but I'd really like to contribute something of my very own."

Charles and Louise both nodded. "I think that's fine. I tell you what. I'll call the head of the women's auxiliary and ask if anything else needs to be done. If so, then you can take care of that. If not, then you can do whatever you want to contribute to our celebration. I can tell you, whatever you do will be much appreciated."

Luke smiled. "Sounds good to me. Just let me know when you find out. I'll need to get things together quickly if I'm to be ready for tomorrow afternoon."

"Will do." Louise grinned. "Now, boys, let's eat."

CHAPTER SIXTEEN

It wasn't until supper that night that Luke found out from Aunt Louise that everything for the celebration had been taken care of. Although she tried to tell him it wasn't necessary to do anything else, Luke felt compelled to do something—anything—to feel like he had contributed something to the event. He tried to get some idea of what the others in the community were doing, but that didn't lead him to any ideas of what he could do. As he retired to bed, Luke was determined to stay awake until he had come up with an idea, no matter what it was or what it entailed.

The sun's light shining through the bedroom window awoke Luke the following morning. Although he'd gotten only four hours of sleep the night before, he jumped excitedly out of bed, threw his clothes on, and stopped only for a moment to look in the mirror and run his hands through his hair for that tousled look, as he called it. The last few weeks had been good to Luke, appearance-wise. He was a little tanner, a little more muscular, and his jet-black hair was in just enough need of a haircut that it had a slight wave to it, making him even more attractive. Not that Luke noticed or even cared—well, maybe a little, since he took the time to shave before trotting to the breakfast table for a quick bite to eat before heading out to conquer the world.

"Uncle Charles, I hate to even ask, but is there any way I can be excused from chores this morning? I need all the time I can get before the celebration this afternoon."

Uncle Charles glanced at Aunt Louise. "What have you conjured up for this boy to do today, Louise?"

Louise turned around from her position by the counter where she was frantically icing her last cake. "Me? I'm innocent, my dear. I have no idea what he's talking about. I figured you did."

Charles shook his head. "All of this is news to me too."

"Hey, hello—I'm over here, people! You're talking like I'm not in the room!"

Charles and Louise laughed, and then Louise replied, "Oh, Luke, you haven't taken a day off since you got here. Go—get out of here. Take care of your business. But can I count on you to help me load all of this up around 2:00? I don't have anything else in town I need to help with until then."

"I'll be here to help you too, dear. Since the fireworks were ordered early this year, I took care of all of that days ago. Now all I need to do is show up!"

Luke stood up. "Thanks, y'all. I really appreciate it. I'll be back to help later then, huh?"

"If you can't get back here, though, don't worry about it. Just look for us both over at the baking tent—Louise will be waiting for the cooking contest results, and I'll be sampling the entries," Charles chuckled. "Now, go have a good time."

Luke headed back to his room and took out his suitcase. In the inside pocket, he had placed some money in case he ever needed any while in Shelby. He put some of the money in his front pocket and then started into town, straight to the mercantile.

The town was already bursting at the seams with people. It was the strangest thing to see such hustle and bustle at 9:00 in the morning. Everyone was excited and busy, and to Luke, it seemed almost like Christmas in the city, although it was a mighty small city, and there was no snow on the ground.

As he entered the mercantile, Luke immediately caught a glimpse of Emily busily helping a customer count out candy prizes for the booth she was sponsoring. Luke meandered around the store, looking at all the merchandise as the lady paid for her purchase and Emily walked her to the door. Emily smiled as she saw Luke. "Hi, Luke. What can I help you with today?"

"Actually, I have a bone to pick with you," Luke stated gruffly.

Emily seemed confused and a little startled. "Excuse me?"

"I said I have a bone to pick with you. I spent most of the afternoon with you Sunday, and you never once mentioned this celebration thing to me. Seems to me like you weren't wanting me to come."

"Don't be silly. Sure I want you to be here—I just didn't think about it with everything that happened that day." As soon as she said it, Emily caught a slight smirk on Luke's face and realized he had been just teasing her. But it was too late. She had told him what he'd wanted to hear without even flinching, and now he knew she cared, even if just a little bit.

Luke beamed. "Well, now do I get another question?"

"You most certainly do not." Emily turned her back to Luke and headed behind the counter. "I've said too much already, and you haven't even been here a minute."

Luke teased, "Oh, come on now. I really came here to ask you a big favor. I really need your help today."

"You've already gotten a favor or two from me. I think it's your turn for a favor, if we're playing fairly."

"Okay, okay. I'll do whatever you need me to do, but first I need your help. Seriously, I do."

Emily shrugged. "I guess it depends on what you need me to do."

"First of all, is there anyone else in the store who can handle things for you? I mean, in order to help me, you have to leave the store. Is that a possibility?"

Emily seemed suddenly anxious. "I don't know, Luke. I don't think it's a good idea for me to be going around town with you. Plus, I need to work, because as you can tell by how I live, I really need the money. And I doubt very seriously that Uncle John will let me off today. He's got his own things to do—and, well, I'm not one he usually bends over backwards for." She headed into the back of the store as she continued, "So, my thought is for you to handle things on your own today. Maybe I'll see you later at the celebration." She turned around and plowed right into Luke, who'd followed her around the counter and into the back of the store. "What are you doing?" she exclaimed.

Luke grabbed hold of Emily's shoulders and looked her squarely in the eyes. "Honestly, I don't know what I'm doing. I know that I've never felt this way before. And whether you own up to it or not, I think you have feelings about me, too."

"Luke, I ..."

"Don't 'Luke' me. For once, just listen. I don't have much experience in this area, and like you said the other day, I know very little about you. But I want to know more. If you'll just trust me a little, I can at least be a friend to you—maybe even more. I'm just asking for a chance. I mean, what do we have to lose?"

Emily looked down. When she made eye contact again, her eyes were filled with tears. "Luke, I like you—I like you a lot. But please believe me when I say that you are much better off not getting involved with me. I carry a lot of baggage, and it's baggage that can't be corrected or let go of and shouldn't be shared with others. In the long run, it's not fair to either one of us."

Luke let his grip go. He turned around, looking for a place to sit. When he found a chair and got comfortable, he leaned over, put his head in his hands, and asked, "So basically, what I'm hearing you say is that I'm not worth the risk. I mean, if you really cared, if you really thought we could have something together, even if only a friendship, don't you think it would be worth the risk to jump at the chance and see where it takes us? I mean, if I've learned anything at all from my father's death, it is to take hold of the opportunities you're given. I mean, yes, I got a second chance with my aunt and uncle by making amends for the mistakes I'd made—thanks to you and your advice, I might add—but that's not always the case. From the time I was old enough to remember, my pa always said, 'When I get this crop in, I'm gonna take your mama to do this or when I sell this head of cattle, I'll be able to afford to do this.' I mean, what he was waiting for never came. He wasn't one of the lucky ones to get another chance. Maybe this, right here, right now, is the only chance the two of us get. I just don't want to have a lifetime of regrets, that's all."

Emily sat down beside him and took his hand. "Oh, Luke, don't you see? This *would* be a second chance for me. I've had one chance already, and I failed. I mean, my luck's already wearing thin. Eventually, you get to the point where you're scared to do anything for fear that your luck may run out for good. I know I can't explain it, but that's just how I feel."

Luke reached over and took Emily's face in his hands. "I don't care what has happened in your past, what secrets you may be hiding, or what unknowns await me in regard to you. I just want to be with you, spend time with you, and at least give whatever this is between us a chance—an honest-to-God, full-fledged, fighting chance. If it's my last chance and I get no more, then I'm a winner whatever happens." As he spoke, he leaned over to her. "I want to *live* my life, Emily, not just sit around and watch as others live theirs."

He pulled her close to him, and then their lips locked. Adrenaline rushed through Luke as Emily willingly responded to him. Nevertheless, as she slowly pulled away from him, she began to cry. "I hope to God I'm not messing up here. My life is so screwed up, I just could never live with myself if I did something to …"

Again Luke's lips found hers as they shared another moment together. Then Luke held her close as she continued to shed tears. He knew that whatever secrets she was hiding would eventually come out and that there may be some issues that would have to be dealt with in the future—but for right now, Luke was content.

CHAPTER SEVENTEEN

Luke's contentment was short-lived as a boisterous voice thundered at them. *"What the hell is going on here?"*

As the two of them pulled away from their embrace, an angry, almost livid, man filled the doorway. Emily's uncle had come back from hearing the gossip at the pharmacy and had caught them in what they had assumed to be a private moment. Although he was small in stature, his voice bellowed out. "Son, you best leave now before you find yourself in a load more trouble than you ever thought you'd be in!"

Luke jumped to attention and tried to explain. "We were just talking, sir."

"Talking, huh? When I came in, there wasn't enough room between the two of you for any discussion."

"Uncle John, let me explain …"

"Girl, of all people, you wouldn't be the one I'd ask to explain anything. I'll tell you this, though. You can get yourself ready to go and get out of here. Your day of work is over. I'd just as soon not see that face of yours again until at least tomorrow morning. Do you understand?"

"Now wait just a minute, sir. That ain't no way to talk to a lady."

"Lady, huh?" Uncle John snorted.

"Yeah, lady—that's exactly what I said," Luke fired off at him. "There wasn't a thing going on here that needs any explanation or apology. Plus, it was between the two of us—not you or anyone else."

Turning to Emily, Luke continued, "Now I expect that an apology is in order for Miss Alderman here."

Emily shook her head. "Oh, no, Luke, Uncle John is just looking out for me. He does so much for me already. Let's just go and do as he's asked."

Luke couldn't believe what he was hearing. "After how he just talked to you—you're going to take it?"

"Yes, Luke, I know my Uncle John—you don't." Turning towards her uncle, she apologized. "I'm sorry, Uncle John. It won't ever happen again."

Luke was stunned. What in the world was happening here? He'd just witnessed Emily being treated by her uncle like some kind of a thing instead of a person; and then, if that wasn't enough, she had apologized to *him* for causing his outrage.

"Luke, let's just do as he requested. Let's get out of here."

Acting like an obedient puppy, Luke followed Emily out the back door and into the alley where her pickup stood idle.

"Please, Emily, explain to me what just happened. How can you stand there and say nothing when he treats you the way he does?"

"How the heck do you know how he treats me?" Emily fired off at him. "As I continue to remind you, you have no idea what goes on around here, and you most certainly have no idea what kind of relationship my uncle and I have."

"Hey, I saw how he spoke to you outside church that day—and then again today. He obviously has no respect for you—or maybe it's for women in general. I don't know. What I do know, though, is that I don't appreciate how he treated you in either situation, and I won't stand for that kind of abuse of anyone—but especially of you."

Emily frowned. "See, this is exactly what I was talking about when I said you would be better off not getting involved with me at all. Luke, let's end this before it even begins."

"No, Emily. You're wrong. First of all, I'm already involved." Then Luke smiled and took her by the hand. Leading her around the outside of the store, he continued, "And, second, I just got my wish. Remember, my whole reason for coming to see you today was to get you to help me with something, but you said you couldn't leave the store. Well, guess what? You've left the store, which means you can do that favor for me now. So come on—let's get this show rolling."

"Wait—Luke, where are we going?" Emily asked.

"You'll see. Just trust me," Luke called out to her. "It'll be the most fun you've had in a long time, I can bet you that."

CHAPTER EIGHTEEN

THE REST OF THE MORNING WAS A WHIRLWIND of activity for Emily as Luke led her through the supply store on a wild goose chase to find the items he thought he needed. On the way back to the ranch where Luke planned to build his booth and get ready for the celebration that afternoon, he explained to Emily in bits and pieces how he'd managed the night before to find out from Aunt Louise what booths were already a part of the celebration and what booths had been suggested throughout the years but never used. He took that information to bed with him and tossed it around until he had decided what he would do.

Emily asked Luke why it was so important to him to be involved in the celebration. He just shrugged his shoulders and said, "I don't know. I guess I just want people to know that I did my share."

"See, that's the difference between you and me. I contributed to the celebration today, too, but you'll never know how—I'd rather do things anonymously. I don't need—nor do I want—any fuss about what I do."

"Yeah, but isn't that part of the reason people do the things they do—for the recognition? I mean, I want to contribute because it's the right thing to do, but I sure as heck don't want anyone else getting the credit for the work I did."

"Everyone's motivation isn't the same, Luke. My satisfaction comes from seeing the results through other people. If I give money to the orphanage, I do it anonymously. Later, I may go visit them. If they each have a new toy or something, I know my money helped provide that for them. And if they're excited about it, I am content in knowing that."

Luke smiled and reached for her hand. "You're a good person, Emily."

Shrugging, Emily replied, "That would definitely be open for discussion with some people around here."

Luke shook his head and let go of her hand. "You shouldn't be so hard on yourself. Give yourself at least a little bit of credit."

"That's easier said than done."

"Yes, but sometimes it's worth the effort to try."

They pulled up to the ranch house, and Louise was there to greet them. "Oh my, it looks as if we have a guest for lunch. Hi, Emily dear. It's so good to see you," she said as she gave them each a quick hug. "Luke, what on earth are you planning to do with all those supplies?"

Luke looked over at his truck where the supplies were loaded on the back. "Oh, you'll see. It's a surprise."

Emily agreed. "He says he wants my help, and I still don't even know all that he's planning."

"Well, you have just about an hour before lunch is served, and you know how I am about having our meals on time," she warned.

Backing up playfully with his hands in the air, Luke teasingly surrendered. "I know, I know. We'll be on time!"

Once Aunt Louise headed back into the house, Luke began unloading the supplies. Emily watched as he laid everything out in the order he would need it. "Oh, so you're a neat freak, eh?" she kidded.

"No, just organized. We don't have a lot of time here, so I'm trying to save as much of it as I can by having all the supplies I need ready for when I need them."

"What can I do to help?" Looking at all that needed to be done, Emily felt somewhat useless.

"Can you write?"

Confused, she asked, "Excuse me?"

"Actually, can you write legibly? I mean, I can write, but not for something like this."

"Mmm, I guess so. I got As in penmanship, if that's what you want to know."

"Terrific! Then grab a can of that black paint over there and a paintbrush from the back of the truck, and I'll show you what to do."

Emily did as she was told while Luke pulled a piece of thin plywood out of the back of the truck and used a saw to cut the 4' x 8' piece in half. He told Emily to paint the words *Dunking Booth* on each piece of board.

As she worked, she continually glanced Luke's way to see him take several two-by-fours and construct the square booth frame. Then, he took two more pieces of plywood, cut them in two, and hammered one piece to the lower back of the booth and two more to the lower sides of the booth, leaving the upper part of each side open.

He took chicken wire and cut it to fit the back, front, and side openings, and then used a hammer and nails to secure each piece to the wood frame. Luke stood back and looked at his work so far. He was pleased it was progressing so quickly. He looked over at Emily. She was finishing her job as well, and it looked like a good time to stop and wash up for dinner.

"Hey, Emily, it's 'bout time to eat—are you at a stopping place?"

"Yeah, just a sec. Let me paint this last letter. It can be drying while we're eating."

Luke couldn't help watching the way she cocked her head as she concentrated. *Man, she's beautiful,* he thought to himself. He watched as she carefully critiqued her work, then reached over and touched up a couple of spots that weren't quite up to her standards. Finally, she stood up, wiped her hands on a rag she'd found in the back of Luke's truck, and pushed her hair out of her face. When she turned to Luke, she was surprised to find him looking at her.

"What?" she asked innocently. "What is it?"

Shaking his head to come out of his self-made trance, Luke said as he walked toward her, "I just can't seem to take my eyes off of you. You know you're amazing, don't you? I mean, when I asked you to paint the signs, I had no idea how talented you were—you've been holding out on me. Now I know there are brains behind that beauty of yours."

Emily blushed. "Luke, I'm beginning to think you're just biased. You see me through rose-colored glasses."

When Luke reached her, he took her face in his hands and gently kissed her on the cheek. "You've got to be the most beautiful thing I've ever seen." He brushed his fingers over her lips and then followed them with his lips. It was a short, tender kiss, not passionate, but full of meaning just the same.

Still holding her face toward him, Luke said, "I do believe I'm beginning to like you, Miss Alderman. Yep, I'd sure say that I am. "

Grinning, he said, "Come on, let's get going. I'm not about to ruin this perfect day by being late for a meal. You've never seen anger until Aunt Louise gets a-going." As Emily considered whether to counter that notion with the fact that she had indeed been the recipient of much more violence than any of Luke's family could ever imagine, the decision was made for her as Luke grabbed her hand and took off to the farmhouse. Instead of worrying about it anymore, all Emily could do was try to keep up with Luke as he pulled her along behind him.

CHAPTER NINETEEN

After dinner was done, Luke figured he still had about an hour to finish things up. He left Emily to help Aunt Louise with the dishes while he headed to the truck to get more supplies. He worked like a madman to construct the final part of the booth—the hinged seat. Luke knew this was the most important part of the whole booth, so he used extra precaution as he connected the seat and the bulls-eye together. He tried it out a few times just to make sure it worked and was pleasantly surprised that it did—more smoothly even than he'd ever expected.

He'd decided to slide the tank through the front opening of the booth and finish setting it up at the actual celebration, since it was ridiculous to fill it with water and then try to transport it. He's already spoken to Frank Cartwright that morning about using some of his water to fill up the tank. Frank was the only other person besides Emily who knew about the booth, and he was ecstatic about it. "Anything I can do to help, Luke, just let me know," he'd said when Luke mentioned it to him. Luke was especially grateful for his hospitality after the confrontation he and Emily had just had with John Crawford. Unbelievably, Emily didn't seem too upset about the episode now. In fact, Luke realized, Emily was actually in better spirits now than she'd been before the argument with her uncle.

Maybe, he thought, *I've missed something.* But once Emily joined Luke again and the two of them finished loading up the truck, Luke watched Emily to see if she might be hiding some of her feelings from him. He saw nothing but a peace about her that in some way was extremely appealing and satisfying to him. As they drove down the driveway, heading into town, Luke put his arm over the back of the seat and gently touched Emily's shoulder. "I feel like

I need to constantly pinch myself when I'm with you—you are just too good to be true, you know that?"

Emily smiled, but then shook her head. "Oh, Luke—if you only knew. You wouldn't think it anymore."

Frustrated, Luke shook his head. "I wish you'd quit saying that!" Swallowing hard and taking a second to calm down a bit, Luke added, "Either you can't stand to take a compliment or something in your past totally spooked you. No matter, I think you're pretty terrific, and I'm gonna keep telling you that, so you might as well get used to it."

Emily didn't respond. Instead she stared out the window and tried to keep her mind on other things. She knew that if she and Luke ever entered into a real relationship, he would eventually uncover the secrets she harbored. But right now she had no idea where this was taking them, and the reality of it all was that she didn't even know Luke that well at this point. She was confused and uncertain as to what she needed to do. One part of her said she owed it to herself to be happy—everyone deserves happiness, and that included her. The other side continued to remind her that she deserved nothing after all the pain and suffering she'd caused. She was torn, and she knew that she would continue to be, no matter what the situation. *Maybe I should just tell Luke the truth. That's probably all it will take to get rid of him. I'm just too chicken to do it,* she thought.

"Are you listening to me?" Luke asked. Emily nodded her head. "Well, I don't know how. I've been justa talkin' and talkin', and you haven't said a word. You seem to be in a world of your own."

Emily smiled. "Sometimes it's easier that way. I'm sorry, Luke, I'll do better." Seeing that they were almost to town, excitement picked up in her voice, and Emily continued, "Hey, look, Luke, we're almost there! This is so exciting—does anyone know what you've planned for everyone? I can't wait!"

With Emily's sudden change of attitude and newfound excitement, Luke grinned as the truck slowly pulled into town. He maneuvered through groups of people to get as close to the supply store as he could. Remarkably, he found an empty space and wheeled it in. The two of them were amazed at the number of people already there. Some were just like Luke—running around, trying to get their booths set up, and buying last-minute supplies. Others were actually visitors who were checking things out, hoping to find some early bird specials or get in on an early booth opening. No matter what the reason, there seemed to be people everywhere. Luke began to worry that he wouldn't have time to set his booth up before the actual carnival began. He ran into the supply place and once more, made sure that it was okay for him to use the water spigot. Once he'd gotten approval, he headed through the crowd to find his booth area. Aunt Louise had already given him a ticket telling him what booth number he was. Now he just needed to find section forty-four so the unloading and setting up could begin.

As Luke searched through the crowds, looking down at the brightly colored flags that displayed the booth numbers, he suddenly found himself face-to-face with Emily's Uncle John. Startled, he drew in a quick breath. Not knowing what to say, he stood in silence. Mr. Crawford did the same, only with clenched teeth. Finally, after what seemed like an eternity, Mr. Crawford broke the silence, but it wasn't pleasant. "Boy, I'll tell you this one time and one time only. What you do is your business, but I'm telling you, don't get involved with Emily. It will lead you into a mess of trouble. I can tell you have a good head on your shoulders, but sometimes women put a spell on us men that's hard to pull away from. Get away from her before it's too late. That's your one and only warning."

As he turned to walk away, Luke found his voice. "How dare you tell me how to live my life? I do things the way I want to, and I certainly get involved with the people I want to be involved with. I don't need you or anyone else to tell me what to do or how to do it. Mister, Emily may let you boss her around, but I won't stand for it. You aren't anything to me, and I don't respect your opinion. So keep it to yourself from now on!"

As he wheeled around to leave, Emily was standing there, arms crossed and tears welled up in her eyes. "Luke, how could you?" she cried. "I told you to stay out of it, and you just couldn't do it."

Stunned, Luke began, "But, Emily, he started ..."

"You know what, Luke? I don't want to hear it. You had to go and let your pride get in the way of a perfectly wonderful afternoon, and guess what? You did it! You ruined it for all of us! Congratulations!" Emily began to cry.

Luke rushed over to her and took her head in his hands, forcing her to look at him and only him. "Hey, hey, wait a minute. Your uncle came to me and warned me to stay away from you. I told him what I thought because I'm not going to let anyone tell me I can't be with you. I don't have much experience in this area, but I sure know what my heart is telling me, and that's that you are the one for me. And if it takes telling someone off or arguing about it or having an all-out brawl, I'll do it just so I can be with you."

Emily continued to look at Luke but couldn't believe what she was hearing. Tears continued to roll down her face, but her face was soft and tender now. She reached up and touched Luke's cheek. "Oh, Luke, I've never had anyone take up for me the way you do. I guess I just don't know how to handle it. And as for my Uncle John, well …" she looked around to see if he was still standing there. Of course, he had faded into the crowd to avoid any further confrontation. So she continued, "As I was saying, as for my Uncle John, he has done a great deal for me, Luke. One day, maybe you'll understand. In the meantime, I thank you for taking up for me."

She leaned up and kissed him softly on the lips. At that moment, she didn't care how many people were standing around or who was watching or what would be said later. In fact, she was just beginning to realize that she didn't care about anything except Luke. As for Luke, he had long since stopped caring about anyone or anything else besides Emily. He was totally entranced by her and falling more and more in love with her each day. In fact, Luke knew in his heart that the feelings he had for Emily were real and true, and he told himself that no one, especially not John Crawford, would get in the way of what he and Emily were experiencing and sharing. *I don't even care what secrets she may be hiding,* Luke thought to himself. *As long as I can be with her, I can handle whatever comes my way.* With that, he smiled down at Emily, took her hand, and led her to the number forty-four flag where they began to work setting up their surprise booth.

CHAPTER TWENTY

Luke couldn't have been more right about the success of the dunking booth. Shelby's Fourth of July celebration had never involved a dunking booth, and the townspeople were thrilled! Men lined up one behind the other, half of them begging to be in the booth, the other half anxious to try their hand at dunking those inside. Even a few women fought for a chance to dunk their men. Emily was amazed at the response. She knew the celebration usually brought the best out of the townspeople, but she never realized how much just a little something extra could do for the hearts of the people. And Luke ... well, she stood in absolute awe of his demeanor with everyone he encountered. He seemed so laid back—laughing and cutting up with the men while at the same time continuing to be somewhat shy but nonetheless polite and sociable to the ladies. Emily found herself spending much of the afternoon just marveling at Luke. She felt herself beam from inside out when he looked over at her. She could feel little hints of jealousy creep in when Luke smiled and greeted other girls their age. She'd never felt this way before—she had never really allowed herself to feel any way about anyone else. And if she let herself think too much about it, she began questioning her feelings and whether she should even let herself get involved with anyone—whether she deserved such a thing, or whether someone else deserved to have to deal with everything she brought along with her. She glanced over at Luke. He was so handsome. Luke looked over and winked at her. She blushed and lowered her gaze. Luke pulled away from his position at the booth and headed her way.

"Hey, you look deep in thought." He took a seat beside her on the pavement. "What's going through that pretty little head of yours?"

She smiled. "Nothing, just enjoying watching you. You're so good at being in the thick of it all. I tend to clam up and shy away in large groups."

"Oh, I'm normally not that good in crowds, either. But I've surprised myself today. I guess this celebration has lifted my spirits and hyped me up a bit. It's been great mingling with everyone today—and hey, the booth. I think it's a hit, huh? You know, you should come try it. I may even climb in there and let you take a nab at me. What'cha think about that?"

Emily shook her head. "Oh, no, I think I'll remain the innocent bystander for now, thank you just the same! But," she added, pointing to the crowd gathering in front of them, all looking their way and calling out to Luke to come change dunking victims, "I believe you are being summoned."

Standing up, Luke grinned. "Guess I'm needed elsewhere." Trotting off, he looked back. "Don't go anywhere, Emily. I'll be back in just a bit, and we'll grab us a bite to eat before the dance, okay?"

As Emily stretched out to relax and wait for Luke, she could see out of the corner of her eye that Louise was heading her way. She sighed. She wasn't really up for small talk at the moment, especially with Louise. It seemed like Luke's Aunt Louise read between the lines entirely too much, in Emily's opinion, and she practically despised having to give out personal information, especially to someone she wasn't quite sure she could trust to keep it to herself.

"Luke ignoring you?"

"Well, I believe he's a little distracted at the moment."

The two women chuckled. "Yep, the male ego. You know why our Luke designed this particular booth, don't you?"

"No, why?" Emily asked.

"Well, let's see. Men love the concept of power. Having the power over someone else—being able to dunk their buddies, in this case—just does something to that testosterone level of theirs. They can't help themselves—the competition, the surge they get, the power. And to be the guy who brings all of that to the yearly celebration—what man wouldn't want to be that guy? Luke will be a local legend for sure. These guys' grandkids will be telling about this, and adding to it, I might add!"

Emily was laughing so hard at the truthfulness of it all that tears were rolling down her face. "Stop, please, I can't take it! You're too funny!"

"Well, you know it's true." Louise handed Emily a handkerchief. "It's so good to see you laugh, child. You should do it more often."

Determined to keep the conversation light, Emily said, "I agree totally. I think I may even be sore tomorrow from this laughing fit!"

Louise patted Emily's hand. "Ah, dear, it just goes to show you that you're too serious too much of the time. Sometimes you just gotta let it go. Nothing you can do about the past, so no sense in worrying about trying to go back and change things. You just can't do it."

Defensive, Emily asked, "Who said I wanted to change my past?"

"Honey, you wear your feelings all over your face. It's obvious to me that you worry most all the time. It bothers me to see you wrestling with everything so much."

Having had enough, Emily stood up and smiled. "You know what? I think it's time to get that bite to eat with Luke before the dance begins. Listen, it was great talking with you."

"Emily …"

"I'll see you later, Ms. Louise."

"Emily—wait, I didn't mean to …"

Emily wheeled around, the smile gone off her face. "Didn't mean to what? Pry? Get me upset? Ruin a perfectly wonderful day?" Swallowing hard, she continued, a little calmer. "Please, I don't mean to be rude, but let me just say this. I do the best I can to get through each day. I don't know much, but I do know that being with your nephew helps me forget all the things I worry about most, and that draws me to him." Backing up, she continued, "So, if you don't mind, I'd like to find Luke now. See you later."

Louise sat down, disgusted with herself. Usually she did much better than that. At the moment, she just couldn't figure Emily out, and she definitely couldn't reach her. "Heck fire, all I've done to this point is upset her and push her away. Yep, I'll just have to try a little harder next time," Louise vowed.

She saw Luke and Emily walking toward the food booths. "At least they're not bothered by others seeing them together." That made her think about her other half. She stood up. She knew he would be hungry by now—but being the man he was, he would be waiting on her to get him something to eat. Shaking her head, she chuckled and headed off to look for him. She may have struck out with Emily, but she most certainly knew how to reach her man—through his stomach.

CHAPTER TWENTY-ONE

The Fourth of July celebration ended as eventfully as it began for Luke and Emily. After an afternoon of fun, games, contests, and good food, the booths became deserted at exactly 8:00 when the entire town gathered at the pavilion for dancing. Luke grabbed Emily by the hand, and like a little kid, began weaving in and out of the crowd, eager to get settled at a good table before the festivities began. Emily giggled as he dragged her along behind him. She felt like someone half her age, and it felt good. Looking around, she saw smiles on everyone's faces—Aunt Louise was grinning ear to ear, because, of course, she was sporting the first place cooking prize once again; women were grinning, holding on to their men as they made their way to the dance; and men were proud of their women, satisfied with the day's competitions, and happy with the full stomachs they each possessed. All in all, it had been a magical day for Emily, as well as all of the townspeople.

The band members were tuning up as Luke and Emily settled down at a cozy table for two. Neither of them knew if the other one danced— it hadn't even been mentioned. But neither cared as they sat, enjoying each other's company and the array of activity surrounding them.

"Welcome, welcome, ladies and gentlemen. There's still plenty of room for those of you just joining us. Move on into the pavilion—there you go. That's right!"

The mayor gave everyone a minute to settle on in, and then he continued. "Welcome, everyone! Today has been a terrific day here in Shelby. I dare say that this celebration has been by far the best one this community has ever had!"

The crowd applauded, and whistles were heard in the background. The mayor raised his hands to settle the crowd. "I'm certainly glad we agree! It has been a day to remember. First I'd like to thank everyone for your continued support and dedication to our town. Without all of you, there would be no celebration, and certainly not the camaraderie we share here in Shelby. Second, I'd like to extend a special thanks to Luke Garrison for his great dunking booth!"

Shouts and cheers erupted throughout the crowd. "Son, you added a special spark to this year's celebration, and we appreciate your efforts. The dunking booth was, in my opinion, the highlight of the event!"

Again, the crowd clapped and shouted in agreement. Luke grinned and nodded his head, completely embarrassed by the attention but loving it just the same. He was ecstatic that his idea had been such a huge success. *Sure wish Pa was here,* he thought, as the mayor continued speaking and the crowd settled down, turning their attention away from Luke. Luke glanced over at Emily to find that she was smiling at him.

"I'm proud of you, Luke. I'm really, really proud of you!"

Luke grinned. "Thanks, but I couldn't have done it without you!"

"What did I do? Anyone can make a sign!"

"Yeah, but I wouldn't have had the will or desire to prove myself if it hadn't been for you. You inspired me."

It was Emily's time to blush as she turned away from Luke. "Oh, look, the dance is starting," she said, as if trying to take the attention away from herself. "Do you dance?"

"Who, me? Ah, I don't really, I mean, I've never, I mean, well—no, I don't guess I do. Do you?"

"I think the last time I ever thought about dancing was when I was a kid. But look at everyone—how hard can it be? Looks like most of 'em are just swaying back and forth with the music."

"Yeah, I guess so. But, I'd just as soon sit here and watch awhile, if that's all right with you."

"Oh, yeah, that's fine with me. Look, there's a lemonade stand the ladies have set up over there. I'll go get some for us."

Emily headed to the table where a few of the ladies' auxiliary members were pouring lemonade. "I'd like two lemonades, please," she said to one of the women.

"Hi, Emily dear." Emily turned quickly to see Mrs. Cartwright standing behind her.

"Hello," she replied with a weak smile.

"I just wanted you to know that I think Luke is a wonderful young man. I can't say I know too much about you, dear, but if Luke likes you, then you must be okay."

Emily smiled and nodded, not knowing what to say. She turned to take her lemonade, and when she turned back around, Mrs. Cartwright was already gone. *She's right,* Emily thought, *Luke is a good man. Too good for me, I know, but maybe it's a sign that I need to start moving on and leave the past behind me.*

"What are you mumbling about? And get that awful grin off your face!" Emily's uncle snarled as he grabbed Emily's arm and pulled her aside. "Don't you realize the pain you've caused? And you still think you deserve to be happy? You're more of a spoiled brat than I gave you credit for. How dare you think so highly of yourself to go and forget all the things you've done!"

"How can I forget when you're constantly reminding me of how much of a lowlife I am?"

His grip became stronger, and Emily winced. "Don't you dare use that tone of voice with me after all I've done for you. You don't deserve him, and he certainly doesn't deserve you! Oh," he mocked, "but, of course, he doesn't know the real you, now does he? 'Course, I can solve that right now, missie!"

"Uncle John, please," Emily pleaded, "I know what I've done, and I have to live with the consequences of that every day of my life. But please, Uncle John, please don't tell Luke. Yes, he deserves to know, but he should hear it from me. He deserves to hear it from me, and you know it. Please, I try not to ask you for much, but I'm begging you now, give me time to tell him myself—in my own way, in my own time."

Dropping his grip, Uncle John smirked. "And you expect me to believe that? From *you?* I tell you what. You have until tomorrow. I'm sick and tired of seeing the two of you together, and I hate to even imagine what's going on with the two of you, but since I expect it to be over as soon as you tell him, I won't have to deal with that picture much longer. So yeah, you can tell him. But you have to do it tonight."

Fighting back tears, Emily begged, "Please, let me tell him in my own time."

"This isn't your call, my dear Emily. Either tell him tonight in your disgustingly toned-down version, or he can hear the real truth from me."

As he walked off into the darkness, away from the lights of the dance, Emily tried to regain some composure. This day had been a day right out of her dreams, but now it was over. Luke would hear the truth tonight, and by tomorrow it would all be over. *So much for second chances,* she thought.

"Hey, beautiful. Where's that lemonade you were bringing me?"

Emily jumped at the sound of Luke's voice, spilling lemonade all down Luke's shirt. "Ah, there it is!" he laughed, trying to rub off the excess as best he could.

Unable to control her emotions, Emily sobbed. "Oh, Luke, I'm so sorry—so very, very sorry. You scared me, and I …"

Luke saw fear in Emily's eyes. "Honey, it's okay—it'll dry. I promise. Please don't be upset."

Emily replied, "I wish that was all it was. Luke, we really need to talk, and I think we need to do it right now. Can we find a quiet place away from everyone? Maybe where we can still see the fireworks, but so we can be alone."

Luke smiled. It was just what he had in mind—to be alone with Emily. But he couldn't help worrying about what Emily had on her mind. It had been such a great day for the two of them. Never in his right mind could he see what was coming.

CHAPTER TWENTY-TWO

"Before I tell you what I must tell you, let me say this," Emily began as she took Luke's hands in hers. She had led Luke to a secluded little patch of trees, several hundred yards from the dance, so they could be alone yet still be able to catch a glimpse of the evening's fireworks display. It was silly, she knew, wanting to see the show. She was certain that once Luke knew the truth, he would no longer want to be with her anymore. But Luke had never seen the fireworks show before, and Emily wanted to share the moment with him so badly.

Several times while walking from the dance, Emily contemplated not even telling Luke—enjoying the night with him and suffering the consequences later when her Uncle John finally found Luke and told him. But each time she thought about not going through with it, she forced herself to keep moving, knowing she had no other choice. Besides, in a strange sort of way, Emily was sick and tired of living a lie. "Anything has got to be better than the burden of carrying these secrets, no matter what happens," she told herself.

"Luke, getting to know you these last few weeks has been wonderful. Part of me wishes it would always be this way."

Unsure of what was to come, Luke asked, "Why can't it be, then?"

"You don't understand, but soon you will. Just be patient with me, because this is a difficult thing for me to do."

The back of his hand grazed her cheek. "Come on, now. It can't be all that bad, now, can it?"

Emily pulled back. "No, Luke. Don't try to make this any easier. Just listen to me."

"Okay, all right," Luke said, dropping his hand. "Let's just get on with it, then. You've got me all worried now. Just spit it out."

Swallowing hard, Emily continued, "Remember when I told you I used to live in Georgia?"

"Oh, yeah—the Indian town."

"Well, the one named for Chief Osceola—right. At that time, life was good. Me and my little brother, we'd roam the backwoods and do all kinds of ..."

"Wait a minute," Luke interrupted. "I thought you said you were an only child."

"I am now," Emily said, dropping her head. "That's kinda where this whole story begins."

"Well, what happened to him? What was his name?"

"I'm getting to all of that. Just hold on. My little brother's name was John Thomas—JT for short. He was named for my dad and my Uncle John—my mother's brother. My mom and uncle were always real close, and Mama was thrilled to be able to honor Uncle John with a namesake."

Emily paused, trying to find the courage to continue. "Anyway, I was five when JT was born, and I loved him from the moment I saw him. I even called him my baby. I'd take his little hand when he got old enough to walk and drag him around with me everywhere I went. Mama trusted me to do everything for him, and I loved every minute of it. Gosh, those were some good times." Emily paused again, as if in deep thought. Gaining her composure, Emily apologized. "I'm sorry, I just don't usually think about all of that anymore."

"That's okay—so far, so good, though, eh?"

"Well, it gets worse, believe me. As I got older and more independent, I wanted to be with JT less and less. I guess that's sorta normal for kids and their siblings, but what do I know? I just remember JT always pleading with me to take him along when I would go places—and, well, he could be such a pest."

"How old were you when you were going places? I mean, you couldn't have been too old."

"I didn't really mean going places, specifically. Just going around. See, we lived around a good many other families, so there were lots of kids my age. We were all little explorers, and none of us were afraid of anything. By I guess seven or eight years old, we were roaming the town of Ocilla, doing what we pleased."

"What about school?"

"Oh, this was during the summer. See, my Mama, well, she was never a strong one. More like a helpless child, most would say. She was scared of her own shadow and couldn't make a decision for the life of her. To be perfectly honest, she may've been strong enough to bear children, but she certainly wasn't strong enough to raise 'em. My father was the only voice of the house—and, well, he worked twelve to fifteen hours a day, six days a week. Sunday was church, and then it started all over again. Papa told me over and over again to not upset my Mama, so I would head out with the other kids each summer morning, come in for lunch, then head out again until late afternoon."

"Sounds like one heck of a childhood."

"Yeah, it was heaven on earth, at that point. Problem was, JT was always tagging along, and by the time I was ten and he was five, it just wasn't something I wanted to deal with all the time. I mean, we all had bikes. His tricycle couldn't keep up. He'd cry; we'd have to wait on him. All my friends would get frustrated, which frustrated me. So eventually we started trying to outrun him. He'd cry for a few minutes but would end up turning around and going home. You'd think he'd have learned eventually, but come the next day, he'd be racing to catch us again." Emily wiped tears from her eyes. "Looking back, it's hard to swallow the fact that we did such a thing, but ..."

"Hey, don't be so hard on yourself. You were just a kid. You didn't mean any harm."

"True, but it still doesn't make it right."

"No, but you can't go back and change it now. You just learn from it and move on."

"I wish that's all I've had to learn from—my life would've been a lot easier just dealing with that." She stretched her legs out in front of her, then leaned back and looked up at the evening sky. "Man, it's beautiful, isn't it?"

Not taking his eyes off of Emily, Luke replied, "Yep, probably the most beautiful thing I've ever seen." He leaned in to kiss her, and Emily felt herself leaning forward, too. As their lips touched, a chill ran down Emily's back, and she felt goosebumps all up and down her arms. As the kiss continued, Luke's arms wrapped around Emily, and their kiss intensified—so much so that neither heard the sound of footsteps coming toward them. In fact, the two continued their moment of passion for several minutes, and when the two finally pulled themselves apart for air, they saw that Uncle John was standing over them.

Emily screamed, and Luke jumped to his feet, furious that their finest moment yet had been sabotaged—and by Uncle John, no less. "Listen, man, I don't know what it is about us that has you so hell-bent on breaking in all the time, but it ain't right, and it's gonna stop—one way or another!"

"You're right about that, boy. It is gonna stop, and it's gonna stop right now, ain't it, Emily?"

Trembling furiously, Emily slowly rose to a standing position. "Please, Uncle John, you said I could have tonight …"

John cackled. "Yes, I did. I said you could have tonight to clear your conscience and tell him. But girl, you ain't got no conscience or you wouldn't have been doing what you were doing. It ain't right, it ain't fair, and it ain't gonna happen again."

Emily reached her hand out and grabbed her uncle's arm. "I was trying to tell Luke. I was."

Shaking his head, he smirked, "Yeah, well, sorry if I just don't believe you, dear. I know looks can be deceiving, but I feel pretty sure I know exactly what was going on here."

Luke intervened. "Now wait just a dad-blasted minute! We weren't doing anything wrong, if that's what you mean. And you have no right to accuse us of anything of the sort."

"Son, you have no idea. Your precious Emily here is a liar, and it's time you knew it. Believe it or not, I'm actually looking out for you."

Sobbing, Emily begged, "Please, Uncle John, please …"

Frustrated, angry, and confused, Luke threw up his hands. "I give up. Nothing either one of you is saying is making any sense to me. Emily, tell me, once and for all, what the deal is—please."

Emily just hung her head, continuing to sob.

"Emily didn't tell you about her little brother?"

"Well, yeah, she told me a little bit about him—he was named after you."

"Yeah, well, did she tell you how she loved him so much, she ended up killing him?"

"What?" Luke cried, bewildered.

By now, Emily's cries were uncontrollable. She fell to her knees.

"Emily, what is he talking about? Emily?"

"Luke, I …" She couldn't continue.

"Poor thing—so hard for her to face the truth," John mocked. "I guess I'll have to be the bearer of bad news for you. See, Luke, your little Emily here not only let her own brother—her own flesh and blood—drown, but she tried to cover it up. JT's death ruined her parents' marriage and pushed her mama over the edge. Yep, this girl of yours ain't no innocent one—nope, she's a murderer, a homewrecker, and not worth the time you've wasted on her."

Unable to take it any more, Emily took one look at Luke's ashen expression and ran away, as fast as she could back through the deserted booths on Main Street and continuing on until she could run no more. Exhausted but still unable to stop crying, Emily walked around to the back of her uncle's store to the truck she'd parked there that morning, climbed in, and drove herself home.

Meanwhile, Luke couldn't comprehend what had just transpired. As quickly as Emily's uncle had appeared, he had disappeared, feeling content that the truth had been told to his satisfaction, leaving Luke with so many emotions and questions he didn't know where to turn or who to turn to.

He dropped to the ground, unable to soak it all in. Emily—a killer? No way. Not his Emily. But why had what Mr. Crawford said upset Emily so? "And why didn't she try to defend herself—if not to him, at least to me?" he asked.

The conversations with Emily that night had made little sense, really. In fact, come to think of it, Emily had been trying to tell him something about her brother. But what was it? Did she really cause his death?

"God, please tell me Emily didn't do this," Luke found himself praying. It had been quite a while since he'd talked to God, but at this point he had nowhere else to turn. "Lord, I know I'm probably not your favorite person at the moment, but God, please help me somehow sort this all out. Show me the truth and help me be able to accept it, whatever it is. Lord, be with Emily. Even if these things are true that Mr. Crawford said, the Emily I know is kind and good and—God, please, don't let her have done these horrible things. Please!"

Luke put his face in his hands and cried as hard and as long as the day he and his Uncle Charles had fought and he'd finally surrendered to the grief of his pa's death. And as the fireworks display began and the end of the July Fourth celebration drew near, Luke found himself more broken, more shattered, and more a mess than he'd ever been.

CHAPTER TWENTY-THREE

"I WONDER WHERE LUKE WENT OFF TO," COMMENTED Louise as she and Charles moved along the dance floor.

"You know, Louise," Charles began as he shook his head, "no matter how many times you ask me, I'm still not going to know where that boy is."

Louise laughed. "Oh, I'm sorry. I just hope he's having a good time. I worry about him so."

Giving her a peck on the cheek, Charles nodded. "I know you do, but you know what?" He took her hand and began to lead her from the pavilion. "Worrying ain't gonna bring you more reassurance, either. He's a grown man, Louise, and I'm sure he's fine, wherever he is."

But as the fireworks began, Luke was still nowhere to be found. Louise couldn't believe he would miss the highlight of the celebration, especially after such a wonderful day. He had been so excited. He'd told her that he'd never been to a real fireworks show before. Louise just couldn't figure it out. "Call it intuition, but I just know something's not right with Luke," Louise said to herself. "He would be here if everything was okay."

Once Louise and Charles had said their goodbyes to everyone, Louise finally got the answer she'd been looking for. As the couple located their truck, Louise looked up and gasped. Leaning against the vehicle in a pitiful, slumped-over way was Luke. His eyes were red and swollen, and his expression was blank—he looked worse than Louise had ever seen him. Rushing over to him, she mumbled, "Oh, I knew it. I knew something had happened." Grabbing him up, Louise led Luke to the back of the truck where Charles was busy letting down the tailgate. Then the two of them helped Luke sit down. Before Louise could ask what had happened, Luke began to weep. Lifting his head a little, he pleaded, "Can you just take me home? Please, let's just go home."

Tears welling up in her own eyes, Louise agreed. "Charles, let's get him home, and then we can sort this whole thing out."

It took only a matter of minutes to get back to the ranch, but to the threesome it seemed like hours. No one said a word the entire ride, and Luke remained slumped over with his head in his hands the whole trip. Charles focused on the road, his grip on the steering wheel getting tighter and tighter every mile of the way. And, Louise—well, Louise wrestled the whole time with her inner thoughts. Scenario after scenario haunted her, and by the time she could see the edge of the ranch, she was having trouble keeping herself intact. Inside, she wanted to scream and shout and beg Luke for the truth—anything instead of having to fight her out-of-control thoughts.

Once the truck had pulled into the driveway, Luke stepped out and slowly headed inside. Louise tried to run after him, but Charles grabbed her by the arm. "Wait just a minute, Louise. Now, I know you want to find out what happened. I do, too. But the boy doesn't need any pressure from the two of us right now. He knows we're here, but you back off and let him come to us."

Jerking away, Louise retaliated, "Now, listen here, Charles. That boy's been through some kind of somethin' tonight, and I most certainly tend to find out what it is. I love that boy dearly, and I deserve to know the truth!"

Again, Charles grabbed hold of Louise. Softening, he said, "Honey, I know how upset you are, but please listen to me. He's been traumatized by something, and if my instincts are right, it has everything to do with Emily Alderman. The last time we saw Luke at the festival, the two of them were together. After that, neither of them could be found. So please get all those ridiculous notions out of your head, because I know you're thinking 'em, and start believing that this is all about a girl. And you know what? I bet it has something to do with that girl's uncle, too."

Louise swallowed, letting what Charles had just said sink in. "You know, I bet you're right. I never saw Emily again after she and Luke left the dance." Determined to help make things right, Louise nodded, as if agreeing with herself. "Well, now, I can definitely help in this area. Step aside, Charles, because all I need to …"

"Louise—"

"… do is get him to …"

"Louise—"

"… tell me exactly what …"

"*Louise!*"

"*What?*"

Charles threw his hands in the air and stubbornly turned away from her. "Will you just listen to yourself? I thought we just agreed we'd let *him* come to *us!*"

"Yeah, well, that was before …" Charles didn't hear the rest of what Louise was saying. She'd quickly gotten tired of the conversation and had taken the first open opportunity she'd had to run for it. As Charles turned back around, the screen door was slamming.

"Good gosh, that woman—stubborn as a mule!" he muttered as he headed up the steps and into the house.

CHAPTER TWENTY-FOUR

Louise found Luke sitting at the kitchen table. He had poured himself some lemonade and was shakily holding the glass in front of him. He was no longer crying.

Charles had entered the house and was heading toward the kitchen when he heard Louise. "Luke," she said softly, "Honey, you know we're here if you need to talk."

Well, I'll be doggone. I reckon she does listen to me sometimes, he thought to himself. He leaned against the kitchen door. "Son, your aunt is absolutely right. We don't want to pressure you, but we are certainly concerned, and we want to be here for you if you need us." He winked at Louise, and Louise blushed, knowing she'd made him proud. They stood in the kitchen, staring at each other and waiting. Finally, Charles motioned for Louise to follow him out of the room in order to give Luke his space.

"Wait," Luke said, setting his cup on the table. "Wait. I think you're right. I do need to talk, and I want to do it now, if that's okay."

"Well, of course it is, dear. We are here to help in any way we can!" Louise and Charles sat down, and Louise reached for Luke's hand. "Why don't you start from the beginning?"

He took a deep breath and slowly exhaled. "Aunt Louise, how much do you know about Emily Alderman and her family?"

"Well," she began, "I know that Emily's mother grew up here. She and her husband—he wasn't from here—moved to Georgia and were gone for a number of years. Emily's only been back here a couple or three years, probably—wouldn't you say, Charles?"

Charles nodded. "That family tends to stay to themselves."

"Yes, they do. They're right peculiar, if you ask me." Charles shot Louise a dirty look as if to say, "No one is asking you." Louise ignored him and turned back to Luke. "Does that answer your question, dear?"

"Well, no, not really. I meant, how much do you *really* know them—you know, their secrets and all?"

Louise looked over at Charles. Charles began to fidget in his chair, and Louise looked a little scared of what was to come.

"So you *do* know more than you're telling me, don't you?" Luke accused, fire stirring in his eyes.

Louise bit her lip. "Now, hold on just a minute. We try real hard not to discuss other people's failures and shortcomings when we have so many of our own—isn't that right, Charles?"

Charles agreed. "Yes, Louise, but in this particular case, I believe the whole truth is rightfully deserved."

Louise nodded, but wasn't happy about it. Her eyes welled up with tears. "Charles, I don't think I can take it ..."

"I know, dear." He interrupted her and took her hand. Softly, he said, "Listen, why don't Luke and I finish this conversation on the porch, and you go on and get ready for bed? The two of us are bound to be up all night—and, well, you need your rest. It's already been a long day."

Louise stood up, kissed Luke on the cheek, and then blew a kiss in Charles's direction. She was thankful she wouldn't have to be a part of such a tragic story, although she knew in her heart she'd lie in bed listening to Charles tell it nonetheless, crying like a baby.

The two men settled on the porch and then sat in silence for several minutes—Luke waiting for the story to begin, and Charles praying for the courage to tell it.

"Son, it wouldn't be right if I didn't start at the very beginning, so just hear me out. You may not think some of it relates, but it'll all come together in the end."

Luke nodded.

"Years ago, when your aunt and me and even your pa were growing up, Jack Hawkins was a good friend to all of us. I told you some about how Jack went after your aunt and was devastated when she turned him down to marry me. He had a hard time getting over the hurt he felt, and he took it all out on me for a while. 'Course, your aunt was definitely worth it! Really, your pa wasn't involved in all of this. He just saw the effects it had on me and Louise.

I remember him saying to me that true friends stick together, and that Jack would eventually come around. And you know, your pa was right. Eventually, Jack did come around. He had found someone else—Grace Crawford—and seemed to be happy again. Apologized to me and everything. I mean, the two of them were joined at the hip, practically."

"Hey, was that Crawford girl any kin to John Crawford, Emily's uncle?"

"Yes, Grace was John's sister, but I'll get to all that. Just hold your horses. Now, like I was saying, Jack and Grace were inseparable. Until one day—and no one really knows what happened—it was over between the two of 'em. And not only was it over, Grace had run off and married another man. To be honest with you, it happened so fast—and of course, so long ago—that I have a hard time remembering." He stood up. "I need something to wet my whistle. I'll be back in just a sec."

While he waited, Luke took a long sip of his own lemonade. So far he was having trouble understanding what any of this had to do with Emily and the death of her brother, but at least concentrating on the story had calmed him down some and was helping him think a little more clearly.

"Yep, Son, time slips past you, and it gets harder and harder to remember all the details," Charles remarked as he closed the screen door quietly so as not to disturb Louise, who was pretending to be asleep. "All right now, where were we?"

Fidgeting, Luke replied, "You were at the part where …"

"Oh, yeah, yeah. I remember. Grace had run off and gotten hitched to someone else. Near 'bout broke Jack's heart. Actually, you know, I guess it did, because as you can tell, Jack ain't never recovered. I always accuse him of having no heart, and really, I guess it's true. Bad things'll make you or break you, so they say, and Jack let it break him. Two heartbreaks, and the man has been bitter ever since. Any harm he can do or any problem he can create, he's on top of it. The man was dealt some bad cards, and he has pounced on the opportunity to use his experiences to make things worse for everyone around him."

"Yeah, but does he do other people the way he does you? I mean, come on, going around cutting fences and stealing cattle? He should be arrested for stunts like that!"

"I agree, but most people don't see that part of him. They just see him as old and crabby and mean. He saves those vindictive things for those who've hurt him the most—me, and your aunt, and in Grace's situation, Jack takes it out occasionally on her brother, John—but really, only when it comes to making decisions about Grace."

"I wouldn't think it'd be too hard for anyone to despise either one of 'em, especially Jack."

"Well, that's where the Lord comes in. See, Son, I tried to hate Jack for a long time, but my heart wouldn't let me. I despise the man's actions, that's for sure; but the man himself I feel sorry for. I know what a great guy he used to be, and it's a pity he has nothing to show for it."

"I don't know if I'm as good a person as you, then. I'm not too good at forgiving."

Charles shook his head. "You got it all wrong, boy. This has nothing to do with being a good person. Believe me, I have some rotten thoughts at times and have definitely made my own share of mistakes. But, well, the good Lord—for some reason—chose to love and care for me, and more importantly, forgive me. He loves me in spite of who I am, and that itself gives me the strength and desire to be a little more understanding of other's situations and actions. I promise you, I see that same thing in you. You've come a long way since your father's death. You're stronger and more together than you think you are."

"I'm glad one of us has confidence in me."

"Well, I do."

"I appreciate that, Uncle Charles. Now, where were we?"

"Let's see," Charles thought aloud. "I told you about Jack. Now, let's get back to Grace. Honestly, I don't know anyone who knows what led Grace to marry that other man—oh, what was his name? Travis ... no, Thomas—that was it! Thomas Alderman. He was smooth-talking, full of himself—a city guy, in my opinion. He rolled in here, took advantage of Grace, and talked her into marrying him. But I'm getting a little ahead of myself. Let me go back to Grace. Grace was always fragile. She was good-looking but never thought too much of herself. She was easily led and was scared to death of her own shadow. Grace was just someone who couldn't take a whole lot—she just couldn't handle a lot of things at one time."

"What exactly was wrong with her?"

Charles shook his head. "Nothing was wrong with her. I mean, she wasn't slow or anything. She was just—fragile, that's all I can say. She never dated much. I guess Jack was really the first to pay her any attention. What is beyond me is how she gave up that happiness—because we all saw it in her eyes—for someone she barely knew. Part of me thinks he came in, flashed his money around, and talked a big game, and she was hooked. Grace's family was very poor, and maybe she thought marrying money and moving out of Shelby was the best thing for her. But then again, Jack had money, too. Oh, I don't know. You know how the pasture's always greener on the other side of the fence, so to speak."

"What did Grace's parents think?"

"Like I said, that family was poor. I think at first they were shocked, but on the other hand, they were hoping she could get away and have a better life than what they did."

It was Luke's turn to stand and stretch. He walked over to the rail and leaned back against it. Yawning, he said, "I bet it's close to midnight already."

"Yep, it's getting close." Seeing Luke's tired expression, he continued. "Son, we can always finish this in the morning. I know you're worn slap out."

"No way! I can't sleep right now if I try. I gotta hear all of it. Let's get on to the part about Emily."

Charles nodded. "All right, all right. I figured you'd say that. Okay, Grace married Thomas, and they immediately moved to southern Georgia. I believe it's where his family was from. Lord only knows what he was doing out here—maybe a hunting trip or something. I know he was some kind of salesman, so I guess it could've been business. I just don't know. Anyhow, they moved away. John, Grace's brother, was most upset about it—besides Jack, of course, because he and Grace had always been real close. John was very protective of Grace, and he wasn't too keen on Thomas. It was almost like he could see right through him, but John never told Grace how he felt. Nope, he loved her too much to upset her. Instead, he supported her even when he thought she was wrong."

"That's some kind of brotherly love, huh?"

"Yep. John kept in pretty close touch with Grace over the next few years. He'd tell people how she and Thomas were doing. I remember how thrilled he was when Emily was born. He had a huge sale at the mercantile and called it the 'Congratulations! I'm an uncle!' sale. Everyone who came in got a free cigar and 20 percent off their purchase. I got a kick out of his excitement. He was even more thrilled when Emily's brother was born. Grace named her baby John Thomas—after her brother and husband—and John was beside himself. Only he didn't have a sale this time. Instead he closed completely down for three full weeks and headed to Georgia for a visit.

"Looking back, I think the birth of JT weakened Grace a good bit, but she loved being a mother. Thomas was thrilled with his children as well, although I believe he loved the fact that he had a namesake a little more than anything else. I really don't know all the details of their years in Georgia, but I do know this. When JT was five, I believe, there was a tragic accident."

"Wait a minute—John claimed that Emily killed JT, and he acted like she did it on purpose!"

Charles look disgusted and then saddened. "You know, Son, when troubles come, it's so dad-blasted easy to blame the ones you love the most."

"So she didn't do it? Please tell me the truth, Uncle Charles! I'm dying to know what really happened!"

"No, Son, Emily didn't do anything. God bless that child; she was just a little girl herself. But now that you know that, let me go back to where I was leading up to."

Luke's expression had totally changed. A calmness had come over him, and a peace had filled his entire body. Knowing that Emily hadn't done what her uncle had accused her of was the news he'd hoped for. Now he could relax a little and try to understand why everything had gotten so misconstrued.

"See, the Aldermans lived in a small town with a good many young children, and all those kids loved to go to a certain swimming hole during the summertime. Emily was no different. And by the time JT was born, Grace had little strength left to deal with the hassles of motherhood."

"But I thought you said she loved her kids?"

"She did. She loved them dearly. She just wasn't strong enough to handle the day-to-day stuff. So taking care of JT fell on Emily. I mean, Thomas worked all the time and was on the road a good bit. Emily, bless her heart, stepped up to the challenge and claimed JT as her own. She would do anything he needed her to do. But eventually, the other kids got tired of being slowed down by Emily's kid brother. They started telling Emily she couldn't go with 'em either if JT had to come along, because they had things to do, and they didn't want to be held up by a five-year-old."

"You really can't blame her, can you?"

"Well, of course not. I mean, she was just a kid, for gosh sakes! That fateful July morning—well, Emily got ready to go out with her pals, and JT was nowhere to be found. She figured he must've climbed in the bed with Grace, which is what he did sometimes. So Emily headed out and never looked back. When lunchtime rolled around, Emily headed home with not a care in the world!"

The screen door creaked, and both men turned to see Louise standing there.

"I thought you were asleep!"

"You know better than that, Charles. I just couldn't stand to be out of the conversation any longer. And I wanted to make sure Luke understood everything."

"Honey, that's fine. Have a seat."

"Thank you. Now go on with the story," Louise said as she settled in for the tragic ending.

"Well, Emily made it home all right, but when she did, Grace questioned her about JT. Surprised, Emily quickly told her that he didn't go with her that morning. Since I don't know all the details, I can only give you the general facts. The two went to search for him. Eventually the whole town became involved in the search. Thomas was called to come home, and the local police began their own search. There was no sign of him until the next day when police found his little body floating in the swimming hole."

Louise cried out. "I can only imagine it was the worst news a mother could hear. When the news reached John and all of us, it was just horrible. Even though I didn't know the child, it broke my heart, because I did know Grace and John, and I just hurt so badly for everyone involved." She put her hands over her face and sobbed.

Charles continued. "It was awful bad around here, so you can only imagine what it was like there. The police labeled it as an accidental drowning and pieced together what they called the facts of the case. According to them, the series of events went something like this: Emily and her friends headed out to the swimming hole, unaware that JT had been hiding out in the bushes, waiting for them to leave. He was a right bit smarter than what they gave him credit for. After the kids were out of sight, JT took his time and followed them. But as all little boys do, he got distracted—by Lord only knows what; it could've been anything. Anyway, by the time he made it to the swimming hole, the other kids had moved on to do something else. JT thought he was old enough to swim with no help—and, well, within a few minutes, he had drowned. Emily was never aware of JT following her until after the fact."

"So if it wasn't her fault, and the police even said it was an accident, why does her uncle blame her?" Luke asked.

"Well, Son, the tragedy of it all is just beginning. Once the investigation and the funeral were over, the rest of the town went on with their lives. That's when the reality of it all hit. Part of the grieving process involves anger, and Thomas had enough anger for everyone. He blamed Emily for JT's death and repeatedly told her how much grief she'd caused him and Grace. As a ten-year-old girl, hearing that makes you begin to believe it, too. And poor Grace—she just couldn't do anything but lie in bed and cry. She became depressed, and instead of fighting to get beyond all that had happened, she just surrendered to it."

Luke couldn't understand it. "Why didn't Thomas find some help for Grace? I mean, he just sat there and watched her suffer?"

"Thomas was suffering, too, but in anger. He decided that he and his family needed to get out of south Georgia and make a new life for themselves. So they moved, and moved, and moved some more. In fact, they lived in several states before Thomas realized that moving wasn't the answer to his problems, either. So, he began having fits of rage, taking it all out on Emily. Then, when he didn't feel better, he turned against Grace as well."

"You mean he became abusive to them?" Luke was getting a little fired up himself.

"Only verbally, but still, that was bad enough. It traumatized both Grace and Emily. And then finally, one day, Thomas just never came back home. He left the two of them. "

"Good riddance!" Luke grunted.

Louise sighed. "I don't know if that was Grace's breaking point or not—if Thomas hadn't left, would she have been better off?"

"I doubt it," stated Charles sadly. "I think Grace was doomed even before that."

"Where did he leave them?"

"I believe it was Oklahoma—right, Charles?" Louise asked.

"I think you're right. With no family, no friends, and nowhere to go, Grace called John. And, well, John brought them back here so he could take care of his beloved sister. And, yes, he had anger, too; and he turned it on Emily. He has always despised Thomas, for one thing, and the only good that came out of the marriage, in his opinion, was his namesake. So when JT died, he went back to the fact that it was all Thomas's fault for taking Grace away from him and everything. Then when Thomas left, he had to blame someone, so he blamed Emily. He told her he'd let her work at his mercantile and pay her only enough to eat and pay rent—to him, mind you, since he owns that dilapidated shack they call a home. And he continues to remind her constantly how she ruined her whole family's life, including his, and how she will work for him her entire life and never be able to fix the damage she's done. Emily believes him, I'm sure."

Louise agreed. "Yes, she does. Poor child, she wrestles constantly with herself about the whole situation. She comes to church, thinking she can pray and repent enough for God to love her again, but what she doesn't understand is that God loves her now. It's that Emily doesn't love herself and can't forgive herself that's the problem. She's just tormented! And it breaks my heart!"

"Sounds to me like she's served her time," Luke said, somewhat disturbed. "I mean, she didn't do anything—we all know that—but she thinks she did, now that everyone's run her in the ground for so long. My argument is: you've done your time, God forgives you. Now forgive yourself. She's got to understand that. I mean, it's just common sense, right?"

Charles disagreed. "I don't know, Luke. It's easy when you're on the outside looking in. But Emily's lived with this for so many years. She can't just decide to forget it and go on now. It just isn't that easy."

"And Luke, dear, you know yourself how you didn't want to go to church with us the first time. You were angry with God for your pa's death. Of course, Emily's not mad, but it's still the same. She's upset and feeling guilty. Letting go of feelings such as that takes effort. You crossed over that point, but Emily hasn't. And just 'cause you want her to doesn't mean she's ready—it has to be on her own terms and in her own time."

"I know all this. But I believe I can talk to Emily, and she'll listen to me."

Charles interjected. "Okay, but you need to be prepared for the fact that she might not be ready to listen to anyone."

Louise hesitated before adding, "That includes you, dear. I don't think you realize the damage Emily has suffered."

Luke stood up, yawning. "I do understand. And I want the two of you to understand that I'm going to see Emily first thing in the morning, and before I leave there, she's going to realize the real truth. Then," he added, "it'll all be downhill from there." He hugged Aunt Louise and shook Uncle Charles's hand. "Thank you both for being here. I don't know what I'd have done without you."

Louise smiled sleepily. "You know we're here for you anytime, dear."

Charles stood, too. "Next time, let's try to do the family meeting thing earlier in the evening, what'cha say, Luke?"

Luke grinned. "What, and miss such a beautiful night sky? Sure makes for better bonding, don't 'cha think?"

Charles lunged playfully at Luke, but he was already in the house, protected by the screen door. "You just wait," Charles kidded, "I'll get'cha. Now, get on off to bed—I need my beauty sleep!"

CHAPTER TWENTY-FIVE

Saturday morning dawned bright and sunny—and awfully soon for the Garrison household after the late hours they'd kept the night before. Not wanting to disturb Luke, Louise and Charles tiptoed around the kitchen, whispering as they ate their breakfast and then put away the dishes.

Luke's door remained closed for the rest of the morning until Louise could take it no longer. She slowly turned the knob and pushed the door open. But instead of seeing a sleeping Luke, she was shocked to see a clear room with no sign of Luke.

"Charles!" Louise cried. By the tone in her voice, Charles knew something was wrong. He came running.

"Louise? What is it? What's wrong?"

Louise just pointed at the empty room, not really able to do anything more. "Well, I'll be. I guess he couldn't stand it; he had to go see her. Wonder what time he got up this morning—or did he even go to bed last night?"

Louise finally found her voice. "Oh, I don't know, but I hope he and Emily can work through this. I just pray Emily's strong enough to face things."

"And that Luke's strong enough to be there for her," added Charles. He reached and hugged Louise.

"Dear Lord, please be with both of them," Louise cried.

CHAPTER TWENTY-SIX

"Lord, please be with me. Help me to help Emily." Luke had prayed these words over and over again on his way to the Alderman home. He had gotten up and headed out early, way before daylight. But instead of going straight to Emily's, he headed out into the pasture, and after parking the truck, walked slowly through the field, trying to sort everything out in his mind. In a way, it all seemed like a terrible dream; but he knew that wasn't the truth. Yesterday had been a day of ups and downs for him, and he was just thankful it was over and a new day had begun. It was a day of possibilities—a day for new beginnings. At least that's what he hoped. He knew he had his work cut out for him, but he was definitely up to the challenge. To him, Emily was definitely worth the fight.

He continued walking through the open field for an hour or more, enjoying nature and its surroundings. Afterwards, he headed into town to the local diner. He'd never eaten there before, but he was starving, and he just didn't want to disturb his aunt and uncle after having kept them up so late the night before. Plus it was still a little early to be visiting Emily.

He was one of only two customers in the diner that morning, and he was thankful the guy sitting in the corner booth wasn't anyone he knew. He wanted to be left alone. He just wasn't up for any chitchat this morning. "Two eggs, over easy, biscuits, and a side order of sausage, please. Oh, and some coffee—make it black."

"Coming right up," the waitress remarked as she wrote down Luke's order. She was in her late forties, not ugly but not attractive, either, and totally focused on her job, not in the least bit interested in conversing with her customers. Luke was thankful she wasn't a flirt like the last waitress he'd dealt with on his trip into this town. He laid his head against the booth's window and closed his eyes. He hoped his uncle would understand when he didn't show up for chores. He felt like he would.

"Two eggs, over easy, biscuits, and a side of sausage?" the waitress asked rather loudly, not sure if Luke was resting or asleep.

Luke jumped. "Ah, yeah, that's mine. And coffee—lots of coffee."

"Got it right here. You can just keep the pot; it don't look like I'll be needing it."

"Thanks."

"Yep—holler if you need anything."

"I will."

The meal was delicious, and Luke couldn't decide if it really was that good or if he was just so tired and hungry that anything would've tasted good to him. He took his time, downing two more cups of coffee, until the diner clock showed it was 8:00. Then he paid his bill and left.

Driving to Emily's, he tried to go over in his mind what he would say. Her truck was in the driveway as Luke pulled up. He was nervous, but anxious to see her. He couldn't believe Mr. Crawford considered himself helping Emily by letting her live here. It was worse than a dump and definitely not somewhere he'd want his loved ones to stay. *Loved ones,* Luke thought. *I forgot to ask Uncle Charles what happened to Emily's mom. Oh well, I'll have all the missing pieces soon enough.* He knocked softly on the door and waited. No answer. He knocked again, this time a little louder. He heard someone moving around inside, but still no one answered.

"Emily," Luke called out. "I know you're in there. Open up!"

"Go away!" came the reply.

"Come on, Emily, I want to talk to you!"

"There's nothing to say," she called back. Luke could tell by her voice that she'd been crying—or still was, for that matter. Hearing her upset pulled at Luke's heart.

"Please, Emily. I know the truth, and I know you didn't do anything wrong. Please, let me just see you!"

Pleading, Emily cried, "Luke, please, if you care anything about me, you'll just go away—please, just go away!"

"Emily, I do care about you, and that's why I'm not going anywhere until you let me in!" Frustrated, Luke shook the door handle, and to his surprise, the door opened. Before Emily had time to react, Luke had entered the house and was standing in front of her.

"What do you think you're doing?" she cried. Luke could only stare at her. She looked terrible—her hair a mess, nightgown still on, eyes red and bloodshot, and face swollen from the tears.

"Emily, I …" He reached for her, but she pulled away.

"I can't do this, Luke—not here, not now! Please, just leave." She was fidgeting and nervous, and Luke realized she was acting the same way she did when he visited her the last time.

Trying to understand her actions, he said, "Emily, look. I don't care where you live or what your house looks like, and I certainly don't care what other people think …"

"Emily!" a voice called weakly from the back of the house.

"Luke, go home—*now!*" Emily looked horrified.

Luke began to realize what was happening. "Oh my gosh! That's your mother, isn't it? She's still alive!"

Emily hung her head as if in pain. "Yes, she is, although she might as well be dead. She has no sense of reality."

"She sounded okay then, just a little weak. Let me meet her …"

"No! You can't—I won't let you!"

Again, a timid voice was heard. *"Emily!* Where's your brother?"

Tears rolled down Emily's cheeks. "See, she lives in another world—one that isn't real. Luke, she doesn't even acknowledge that JT is dead. She's blocked out the memory of all of it." She hesitated, then added, "Sometimes I wish I could block it all out."

Luke pulled Emily to him and consoled her. "Emily, I want you to listen to me." He pulled back from her and then put his hand under her chin and raised her head so she would have to look him in the eyes. "I stayed up last night until midnight or longer, talking with my Aunt Louise and Uncle Charles. They told me everything—or at least everything they know about what happened. JT's death wasn't your fault. His death was an accident, and you have to start believing that!"

"You don't get it, do you, Luke? If I'd have done what I was supposed to in the first place, JT would have been with me that day—not hiding out, trying to follow us. I was a spoiled little brat, and I didn't care enough about my little brother to watch after him. And because of my selfishness, JT drowned. The police may have ruled his death an accident, but that accident was caused by me not doing what I was supposed to. Luke, whether you like it or not, irresponsible actions have consequences. JT's death led to my father leaving and to my mother's mental breakdown. And all of that goes back to me. I told you before how important it is to right a wrong if you can, because sometimes, life doesn't give you that chance."

Luke realized he was crying, and he moved his hand from Emily's chin to wipe his tears. Emily's head dropped. It was then that Luke realized what Aunt Louise had been trying to tell him. Emily wasn't ready to forgive herself, and he couldn't make her ready. She would have to come to terms with it all on her own.

Dejected, Luke managed a smile. "Emily, listen. I care about you a great deal, and I believe in you. I want to be here for you if you'll let me, but if you'd rather work this out yourself, I'll respect that, too."

After a moment of silence, Emily answered him. "Luke, I care about you, too. But this is something that happened a long time ago, and I carry around a lot of deep wounds because of it. I have daily reminders that don't really allow me a chance to move on—my mom, my Uncle John. And as sweet as your offer is, this has nothing to do with you. It's something I have to work out on my own and with the little bit of family I have left." She took a deep breath, then continued, "I will tell you this, though. Gettin' to know you has made me want to deal with all of this and work it out so I can finally move on. I've never had that desire before."

Luke put his hands in his pocket and shrugged. "Well, that's a start, I guess. Listen, Emily, I'll let you deal with this alone, but only because you are asking me to." He turned to leave but then thought better of it. "Emily," he said, "please know that I am always here for you. I'll give you some time, but I'll be back to see you and check on you soon. You may doubt yourself, and even others in your life, but you need not ever doubt my feelings for you." He kissed her gently on the cheek and headed out the door, pulling it gently closed behind him. As he backed his truck up in the driveway, Emily fell to her knees and sobbed.

"Emily, where's JT? I can't find him!"

As she heard her mother's voice, she put her head on the hardwood floor, covered her ears, and cried even harder.

CHAPTER TWENTY-SEVEN

SUNDAY CAME AND WENT WITH LITTLE NOTICE. LUKE, along with his Uncle Charles and Aunt Louise, attended morning and evening church services, but no one said a word there or back. Charles didn't comment on Luke missing Saturday chores, and Luke didn't offer any explanation, either. It was just understood between all of them that Luke had gone to see Emily and then spent the rest of the day to himself, and for some reason, that seemed to have taken priority over anything going on at the ranch.

Luke spent most of Sunday afternoon wandering between his room and the front porch. He couldn't say at the end of the day that he was happy about things, but he did feel a peace about the whole situation. Luke had never claimed to be a particularly righteous man. Church was just something his parents had made him do as a child. And really, this summer had been much of the same. He went to church because his aunt and uncle told him to. Then when he met Emily, he wanted to go only to see her. *These were not really the thoughts of one who is righteous,* Luke thought. But then again, he reckoned God hadn't completely given up on him, because he was getting these peaceful feelings pretty strongly and as bad as things were at the moment, Luke felt okay.

Sunday turned into Monday, and Monday slowly led into days and weeks of not seeing or talking to Emily. After two weeks, though, of working each day, attending church on Wednesdays and Sundays, and seeing no sign of Emily, Luke's peaceful feelings were being replaced by those of regret, sadness, and longing. Luke worried about Emily and how she was handling everything. The word was that John Crawford had taken it upon himself to "share" the family secret with anyone and everyone. In his mind, he had kept quiet too long and had decided it was high time people knew the truth about his life and his sister's life. Luke knew Emily hadn't been back to work since the celebration, but only because his uncle had told him so from the talk he'd heard around Shelby.

Word on the streets of Shelby was closer to the truth than Luke had thought it would be. People were saying that a terrible tragedy had occurred when Emily was small and that her little brother had drowned. For some reason, they said, Emily had taken the blame for the accident. Some were even taking sides—there were those who thought Emily should take at least some of the responsibility since she was supposedly looking out for her brother that day, and then there were those who felt that John Crawford was the one to blame in that he was not only out of line to blame Emily, who was just a little girl when it happened, but that he had also been verbally abusive to her ever since Emily had come into town. Of course, these rumors weren't discussed with Luke; instead, Louise overheard the stories at the beauty shop and the grocery store, while Charles dealt with them at the drugstore and the supply store. People talked about it in Charles and Louise's presence—not directly to them, but loud enough for them to hear. And it was done intentionally, only to see if they could get more of the story from either of them. But those who spoke were wrong. Charles and Louise both were quiet about all of it—the accident, who was to blame, the relationship between Emily and Luke, and the night of the celebration. It was so hard for them to deal with seeing Luke in such pain and agony that they weren't about to cause more trouble.

Luke had mixed emotions about his aunt and uncle being so open with him. Of course he was curious about what the townspeople were saying. But at the same time, knowing that Emily seemed to be the topic of conversation in all the local hangouts made him worry about her that much more. Was she still having to deal with her uncle's bullying, and if so, how was she dealing with it now that the truth was out—better or worse? And if she wasn't reporting to work, like everyone was saying, what was she doing? How was she paying for food? Was she able to pay her bills? As Luke continued to let his mind run away with him, he began to panic about Emily and her situation. At times he thought he would absolutely lose his mind if he didn't get to see her soon.

Finally, Luke could take it no longer. It was after church services on Sunday—the third Sunday, actually, since he had seen Emily. The preacher had talked about forgiveness and how people should forgive each other as well as themselves. Luke found himself listening intently to the message. Then, like a ton of bricks, it hit him. Now was the time for him to take action. He had to see Emily—to talk to her, to tell her how he felt, to tell her she had to forgive herself, and to work with her through all of this so they could be together.

He had tried to do it before, when he went to her house a couple of days after the celebration, but he had failed. This time, though, Luke was determined to succeed. Even before the last song was over, Luke began making his way out of the pew, going opposite of the invitational call. Louise reached for him, but Charles stopped her. "Let him go," he said quietly.

"But ..." came her reply, although she lowered her arm just the same. She certainly didn't want to cause a scene in church, of all places. Luke certainly didn't need that to deal with.

What Luke did need, however, was a way to get to Emily. When he'd rushed out of the service, Luke's mind had been racing so that he didn't even consider the fact that he'd ridden with his aunt and uncle. "Going somewhere?"

Luke jumped. The voice behind him startled him and made him think, for a brief moment, that he was hearing things. Turning around, though, he discovered that he was definitely in touch with reality.

"Wh-what are you doing here?" he asked.

"Actually, I came to see you."

"Why?" Luke was obviously baffled by this encounter.

"I think we need to talk."

Luke fidgeted. He didn't quite know what to say or how to proceed from here. Maybe it was just pure luck or circumstance or something, but the very person he was determined to see today was now standing in front of him. Emily had come for him.

"I-I don't know what to say—I was leaving church to come see you."

Emily remained short and to the point. "I figured as much."

Luke took a step toward her. Emily took a step back. "Let me just lay out my boundaries to you so we're both clear. All I want you to do at this point is listen. There are things I need to say to you, but I can't do it with you talking or interrupting. I got my truck over there. If you'll be so kind as to take a ride with me, we'll find a place out of the way so I can get all of this off my chest."

Nodding but saying nothing, Luke followed Emily to the truck. He noticed that, even as worn out and ugly as it was on the outside, the inside had been kept clean and tidy. Luke wasn't really surprised, since it was Emily's truck—that was just typical of her to be neat and orderly.

Neither of them said a word as they drove out of town toward County Road 57. There was a fishing hole out there, but Luke had never had the privilege of visiting it; he'd spent all summer working. He doubted Emily would take him there, anyway. Sundays were sure to bring avid fishermen to the hole, and he knew how Emily felt about crowds, especially now that her secret was out.

But Luke was wrong. Emily headed directly to the fishing hole and parked—not away from everyone, but right between two other trucks. It was as if she wanted to be seen—or she wanted to avoid being alone. Luke couldn't tell.

As she turned off the ignition, Emily turned to face Luke. She cleared her throat and then began to speak in a slow, somewhat monotone voice.

"Luke, I've had a great deal of time to sort things out over the last few weeks. I've spoken with Uncle John at length …"

Luke grunted and shifted in his seat.

"… and I've made some decisions. First and foremost, my mother—well, there's no use beating around the bush. My mother has lost her mind, for the most part. She has no sense of reality and still lives in a world where JT is living and my dad is still around. Keeping her in that house with me was my decision, and it was the wrong one. I guess I wanted to try and make her well, but it just put more strain on me and didn't help her at all. Uncle John is working to get her in a mental hospital in Bozeman—it's the best one around. And Uncle John has offered to pay for her care, which is incredibly generous of him, considering the circumstances."

Again, Luke fidgeted. On one hand, he wanted to smile because Bozeman is where Luke was from, which would mean Emily's mother, and possibly Emily, would be moving to Bozeman. But on the other hand, this wasn't the Emily Luke knew at all. In fact, it almost sounded as if Emily was trying to convince herself more than she was trying to convince Luke. But out of respect for Emily's request, Luke remained silent and let her finish.

"Okay, so then, second, I've decided to find another job. It's not a good idea to continue working for Uncle John—he certainly doesn't want me there—so I'm planning to start looking for something else immediately. Maybe the supply store needs someone—or the pharmacy or somewhere. I have experience. I'm sure Uncle John will put in some words for me. And," she paused, "the sooner I find something, the better. I could sure use the money, that's for sure."

Luke had had just about enough. The more Emily talked, the madder he got. But before he unloaded his anger, he wanted to see what Emily had decided about him—he knew it was all coming down to this.

"Then, finally, you and me." Luke could tell Emily immediately began to soften. "Luke, I guess I care about you more than anyone I've ever met. You have been kind to me, which is something I'm not really used to, and frankly, I've stunk at accepting that kindness. I've treated you terribly at times, pushed you away, given you more problems than you deserve, and you've still chosen to see through all of that to the real me. I don't know why, but I'm thankful just the same. You are a kind, decent human being who deserves much more than me. But as scared to death as I am about trusting anyone, I trust you."

Luke could feel all of his anger slowly begin to drain from his body as Emily stopped, took a deep breath, and continued. "You've treated me with respect and kindness—and, well, love." Emily looked deep into Luke's eyes as she said it, and her own filled with tears. "I'm hoping that, even after everything that's happened and all you know about me now, you will still give us a chance. I've fallen in love with you, Luke, and I pray that you'll be here to help me—help us—through all of this. I need you."

Luke felt like shouting. He felt like crying. He had so many emotions flowing; he honestly didn't know what to do. He looked to Emily for direction, and from there, everything fell into place. Time stood totally still as their lips found each other, their arms locked, and the two simply fell into tune with the other's embrace. Neither cared who was watching, or if they were making a scene. Nothing mattered anymore except the two of them.

For the rest of the afternoon, people came and went from the fishing hole, but Luke and Emily never noticed. They spent their time holding each other, determined to treasure this time—this relaxed, non-controversial time they knew would most definitely never last. For as soon as they were back in reality, it would be an uphill battle. Emily had a lot to deal with, and Luke would have to remain involved, providing the comfort and support she needed to get through it all. It would be tough, and it would be an ordeal—but that afternoon, Luke and Emily made a pact to stick together and work through it all, no matter what.

And as Emily finally put the truck into gear to head home, she was content. She felt as if Luke was, too, by the way he'd responded to her after she'd revealed to him her decisions. Unfortunately, that was not the case. Luke was still focusing on the earlier conversation with Emily, where she'd continually mentioned Uncle John helping her. Luke wanted to help Emily and her mother more than anything, but he needed more answers first. He needed to know why, after all John Crawford had done, was Emily still taking up for him or listening to him at all, for that matter? The first thing he vowed to do was get John out of all of their lives—for good. And, the sooner, the better. He reached for Emily's hand and instantly gained confidence in his decision. *Yep, if I'm gonna protect my girl,* he thought, *hmmm, my girl, I like the sound of that, then Uncle John's gotta go. And that's final.*

CHAPTER TWENTY-EIGHT

Monday morning began cloudy and gray, with threats of rain in all directions. Luke's mind remained on the fact that he had to get Emily's Uncle John out of their lives for good, but he just couldn't figure out how yet. He reckoned he'd have to go have a really convincing chat with him—maybe throw in some threats or something, although he didn't really want to go to that extreme. But for Emily, he'd do it just to give her the freedom she deserved. Plus, with John out of the picture, that left more room for Luke in Emily's world. And that, to Luke, was worth a couple of arguments with John Crawford.

As Luke and Charles busied themselves with the morning chores, the clouds continued getting worse as the winds picked up and began blowing debris around the field. Charles told Luke to get a move on, and the two were just finishing up and heading back from checking the herd when the bottom fell out.

"Well, land sakes! Hold on now. Let me get some towels; you're dripping all over the place!" Louise exclaimed as Charles and Luke burst through the door. She grabbed a couple of towels from the bathroom and tossed them in their direction. "There now. Dry yourselves off and then head on into your rooms and get out of those clothes."

Having been given their marching orders, Charles and Luke made their way into their respective rooms for a quick change of clothes. Afterwards, the three of them contemplated sitting on the porch to watch the downpour but quickly changed their minds as the rain became heavier and the winds picked up enough to splatter water all over the porch as well as the rocking chairs occupying it.

Uncle Charles turned the radio on to hear what the weather reports were saying. Tornadoes had been spotted in various parts of the county, and warnings were to remain for most of the day. Luke briefly considered driving over to the Alderman place to check on Emily but decided against it as the weather continued to worsen. He realized his talk with Emily's uncle would have to wait another day or two; he had no choice because of the weather.

Within a matter of minutes, the electricity went out, and Louise began scrambling around the kitchen for matches and candles. Even though it was midmorning, the storm clouds had darkened the sky to such an extent that it was difficult to see. Luckily, Charles had just replaced the radio batteries the week before, so the weather reports were uninterrupted by the power outage. Luke felt himself getting a little nervous as Charles and Louise continued gathering supplies and checking doors and windows. He stood helpless in the doorway of the kitchen, not knowing what to do.

"Is there something I can help with, Unc?"

Charles only shook his head as he continued his work.

"I—I'll be glad to help."

Charles didn't respond.

"Honey, we're just keeping busy, mainly. There's really nothing to do. Just sit and wait it out is all." Louise put the supplies she'd gathered on the table and took three glasses from the cabinet. "It won't be too long before the heat will take over in here—might as well enjoy some cold iced tea."

"Sounds good, dear," Charles said, taking a seat. Luke followed Charles's lead, as did Louise. And for the next hour or so, the three of them sat, waited, and listened. Then, as if automatically, the storm seemed to lessen and no sound was heard. Luke was just about to breathe a big sigh of relief when, all of a sudden, Charles jumped up.

"Tornado! Tornado's coming!"

Stunned, Luke asked, "What? The storm's almost over."

Louise jumped up, and Luke could see fear in her eyes.

"Come on—into the hallway!" Charles yelled. "Move it, Luke!"

Charles closed off all the doors, and the three huddled in the hallway. There was still no noise coming from outside, and Luke was beginning to feel a little silly about this whole charade. He wondered what his mom would do in this situation. In fact, he wondered how she was doing in general. It had been over a week since he'd talked to her last, and he wondered if she was still getting along okay. He made a mental note to call her after the storm was over.

Luke continued his thoughts as the storm outside grew louder. Eventually it sounded as if the railroad tracks were right outside the house and a train was passing by. Luke began to realize his uncle had some sense after all, because knowing there were no railroad tracks anywhere around, Luke knew that the noise he was hearing was the sound of a real tornado. Now he understood the urgency in Uncle Charles's voice and the fear in Aunt Louise's eyes. He looked over at both of them. The two were holding hands, praying together quietly. Luke could see and feel the love the couple had for each other. He knew that for them, whatever happened would be bearable as long as they had each other. Luke thought back to Emily. He loved her so much and found himself praying that one day they would have the same kind of committed relationship as his aunt and uncle. He prayed for God to look after Emily through the tornado and to give her strength to get through this ordeal. He didn't know where it was all coming from, but the words were silently pouring out of him at a rapid pace. Once he finished praying, he continued to sit, eyes closed. He felt an inner peace come over him that he hadn't felt in a very long time, and he knew the Lord was working within him. He welcomed the feeling and hoped it was the beginning of all good things for him, although he knew that wouldn't exactly be the case. But for the present time, he enjoyed the moment of peace he'd been given.

Outside, as windows began to shatter, shingles were torn off the roof, and tree limbs were broken and strewn throughout the yard, the eye of the tornado ripped straight through the Garrison ranch. Inside, though, it was difficult to detect any turmoil for all three Garrisons remained on the hall floor, hands folded, eyes closed, peacefully in prayer.

CHAPTER TWENTY-NINE

ONCE THE STORMS ENDED AND ENOUGH TIME HAD passed that Charles was certain the end had come, he stood up, nodded his head, and remarked, "All right—the worst is over. The damage has been done. Now let's go and see what work needs to be done."

As the hall doors were opened, blinding sunlight streamed in on the threesome, and it took a few seconds for their eyes to adjust to its brightness. In the kitchen, glass was everywhere. Both windows had been smashed, and little bits and pieces were all over the place. Coupled with the fact that everything on the countertops and table had been thrown across the room, the place was a complete mess. In the living area, less damage was done.

"It must've passed on the north side of the house," Charles assessed. And he was right. After a more thorough inspection, all but one window on the back part of the house had been shattered. The kitchen, laundry room, bathroom, and master bedroom suffered, but nothing really proved irreplaceable. And everyone acknowledged how blessed they were.

As Louise began sweeping up glass, Charles and Luke headed outside. As suspected, the south side of the ranch which, luckily, housed the barn, the tool shed, and the majority of the equipment showed little wear and tear. The yard was a mess with limbs and debris everywhere, but other than that, things were okay.

As for the north side, the damage was worse. A new lawnmower would be needed. Louise had parked the push mower beside the large oak tree, and little was left of either now.

"No big thing—we've been needing a new one anyway," mumbled Charles. Turning to Luke, he said, "We should be so thankful. Son, we could've had it lots worse. This is nothing, really."

Luke agreed. "Yep, a little yard cleaning, and it'll all be good as new."

"Yoo-hoo—ya'll come on in here!" Aunt Louise stood on the porch, calling the two men. "Do ya know what time it is? It's after three o'clock! Get in here and let me fix you up something to eat before we start the cleanup. You must be starving!"

Charles and Luke didn't argue. They headed inside, quickly washed up, and sat down for a quick mid-afternoon snack. They were surprised at what Aunt Louise had already accomplished. The table and chairs were clean, as were the cabinets and floor. She'd swept all the glass and broken dishes into a pile by the door. Besides the broken window and the bare countertops, it was hard to see that anything had even happened.

And by the time darkness fell, the yards were pretty much back in order as well, except for the larger oak tree limbs that had fallen. They would have to be dealt with later. The other limbs, debris, lawnmower, and bags of trash from inside the house were all loaded on the back of Charles's truck, ready to be taken off and burned. The electricity was still off, so supper consisted of cold cuts and sandwiches again. But no one seemed to mind. In fact, no one said a word as they ate and then quickly straightened up after the meal. It had been a long, draining day, and everyone looked forward to turning in for a good night's sleep.

Once in bed, Luke again thought of Emily. He was glad the storm wasn't as bad as they'd thought, and he figured he'd go see her tomorrow to help with her own cleaning. Little did Luke know that cleaning up was the last thing on Emily's mind.

The call came early the next morning while Charles and Luke were out doing morning chores. It was Mrs. Cartwright calling on the church prayer chain. When anyone was sick and needed special prayer or if a death occurred in the community, one of the ladies of the church would start calling others to pray. Mrs. Cartwright always called to inform Aunt Louise, who in turn passed the news along to Catherine Prescott, the church choir director, who then passed it on again until all the church families were informed. Although the news was usually not good, this time it was particularly dreary.

Louise had no idea how she would handle the task before her. But as the men headed back in the kitchen, Louise swallowed hard and began. "Sit down, both of you. I have some disturbing news for you." The men looked at each other and sat down with not a word. "Apparently the tornado made more of an impact toward town than it did here. Luke, Honey, the Alderman place …"

"Oh my God! Where's Emily? Is she okay? Is she hurt?" Luke cried out, jumping to his feet.

"Whoa, whoa, she's okay, Luke. She's okay." Aunt Louise placed her hand on Luke's shoulder and coaxed him back into his seat. "I mean, I say she's okay. Luke, the Alderman place was completely destroyed."

"Destroyed? As in—how bad?"

"As in completely destroyed. You know what a rickety shack they lived in. It just couldn't hold up against the weather."

"Poor Emily …" Luke shook his head.

Louise glanced at Charles for support before continuing. "That's not all, Luke. The worst part is this. Emily was on her way home from town when the storm hit. The weather was so bad she ended up pulling off the side of the road until the storm lessened. When she finally made it home, the scene was devastating. The house was destroyed and, well, Mrs. Alderman—well, she didn't make it, either."

Luke was horrified. He didn't know what to say—or, more importantly, what to do. He looked to Louise for guidance.

"Honey, Emily needs you now more than ever. You probably need to get on over there. I'll get some things together that Emily may need and meet you over there a little later. Go on, now—put a move on."

Luke was in a daze. He'd never met Emily's mom or even seen her, but she'd been a large part of his and Emily's conversations lately, and he knew she was the center of Emily's world.

"How in the world was Emily handling this, and why didn't she let me know about this last night? Not only that, but why does this have to happen now on top of all she's already dealing with? I mean, how much can one person take?" Luke asked. He knew that Grace and her condition had been somewhat of a secret, and a lot of people didn't even know she was back living in Shelby. Luke wondered how Emily was handling that on top of everything else.

Suddenly yesterday's peaceful calm seemed like another lifetime, and Luke once again battled feelings of helplessness, sadness, and confusion. All thoughts of getting back at John Crawford for his treatment of Emily over the past few years were set on the back burner. Luke realized that it wasn't the time or place to deal with anything like that. Instead, he focused his thoughts solely on Emily as he made his way to the Alderman home—or what, if anything, was left of it.

CHAPTER THIRTY

Nothing could have prepared Luke for the devastation and destruction he saw when he drove up to the Alderman place. What was once a rinky-dink shack was nothing more now than a huge pile of wood. Trees were down all over the place, and it was like winding through a maze trying to get down the dirt driveway. The junk that once filled the Alderman yard was gone, but not completely. Instead, it had been moved from its original position to places farther from the house and closer to the woods.

Several cars were parked beside Emily's truck, including that of the county coroner, who'd come back to finalize Emily's mother's arrangements, and that of John Crawford, who, of course, was involved in his sister's affairs as well. The other cars were not recognizable to Luke, although they more than likely belonged to local neighbors and friends, since according to Charles and Louise, Grace was originally from the Shelby area.

Luke parked the truck and headed off to find Emily. He found her in deep conversation with her uncle and decided to let her be for a few minutes. He wandered aimlessly around, analyzing in his own mind the events that occurred the day before and how all of it led to the death of Grace Alderman.

"Terrible tragedy, eh?"

Luke turned around to see an older man, more than likely in his seventies, standing there watching him. His hair and mustache were white with remnants of gray in them. He wore glasses and stood just a little bit hunched over. Luke asked, "I'm sorry, sir. Were you talking to me?"

"Ah, yes. I believe I was. It's sure a terrible tragedy—Grace's death and all. Then again, it was a blessing of sorts, too. She led such a tragic life. She's certainly better off now."

"That's what I hear. I never met her."

"Well, that's a sure shame. Grace was a sweet lady who just couldn't handle the curves life threw her. To be honest with you, I had no idea Grace was even back in town." He shook his head. "She'd been better off staying here and marrying Jack instead of running off with that 'ole Georgia big shot."

Luke was puzzled. "You mean Jack Hawkins—that man? How in the heck would she have been better off with him? From what I know about him, he's pure rotten!"

The man held up his hand. "Son, you're speaking out of turn. Never judge a man unless you know where's he's been and how he got there."

"I believe I know enough about him to be able to …"

"Son, I disagree with you. See, the man you're speaking about is my son—my own flesh and blood."

Luke lowered his head in embarrassment. "Oh, sorry, sir. I should've kept my mouth shut."

The old man shrugged then stuck his hand out. "The name's Lawrence. Lawrence Hawkins."

Luke cautiously extended his hand. "Good to meet'cha, sir. I'm Luke Garrison. I've been staying with my uncle and …"

"Boy, you hadn't learned the ins and outs of this town yet, now, have ya? I know 'xactly who you are and why you're here. You're coming here's old news."

Luke chuckled. "Yeah, I forget sometimes that the outsider is known by all. I still can't remember half the names of the people I've met since I've been here."

"Well, you'll learn. Don't mind that all that much." Mr. Hawkins could see Emily finishing up with her uncle and getting ready to head their way, so he quickly added, "Son, my Jack ain't as bad as you think. Years ago, his heart was broken, and just like Grace, he just never recovered—although they each dealt with their losses in different ways. Despite the hard shell he shows the world, he does have a heart, although somewhat hardened at times. Why, who do you think helped Emily and John take care of Grace all these years?" Shaking his head, he added, "Yep, Grace was the love of Jack's life, even after all that happened between 'em."

Luke swallowed hard, as if trying to understand all that he was being told. "I just had no idea. I thought …"

The old man interrupted. "Hopefully this will be a good lesson for you. You just never know what others are dealing with, so it's best not to judge. It'll just get'cha in trouble."

"Lesson learned," Luke said, still shocked at the information he'd been given. "Thanks for filling me in on some things."

As Emily approached the two of them, the old man quietly made his departure. "Good to meet'cha, Luke. Take care." And he was gone.

Luke turned to see Emily standing there. Her face was red and swollen, and she looked pitiful. Without another thought of his conversation with Mr. Hawkins, Luke instinctively reached out and pulled Emily to him and for the next little bit, held her as she released all her emotions to him. He said nothing to her—he didn't have to. His strong arms holding her said all she needed to hear, and that was enough.

When all the tears were gone, Emily pulled back a little and took a deep breath. She was completely exhausted, but she knew the worst was yet to come. She wasn't too concerned now, though, because she knew that with Luke by her side, she could get through all of it.

"Luke, thank you for coming."

He smiled at her. "You know there's nowhere else I'd be right now. My place is here with you."

Emily let go of him and reached for his hands. "I'm so glad. Listen, Luke, I know you probably have to get back to work. I certainly don't want to keep you."

"Now, don't you worry your pretty little head about that. I'm here with you as long as you need me. In fact, Aunt Louise was getting up some things you might need and is planning to meet me over here."

Tears welled up in Emily's eyes again. "Oh, Luke, look at my house. I don't have one anymore. I've been so busy thinking about Mama that I hadn't even considered that I've lost everything!" She began to cry, and Luke drew her to him once more. "I have no clothes, no money, no place to sleep, nothing. 'Cept that old piece of junk truck. And it's not worth the gas that goes in it."

"Oh, Emily, I'm so sorry—so very sorry. I wish I could do something to take all this from you." Anger rising in him, Luke added, "I just can't understand why God lets bad things happen, especially when you've been through so much already."

Emily jerked her head up and wiped her eyes. "Now, wait a minute. Just because bad things happen doesn't mean that God lets them happen or that God does it to us. Bad things just happen, Luke. It's God, though, who's there to help us through. Always think of God in the positive; otherwise it's tough to understand anything!"

'Well, it's good to see you still have your spunk," Luke commented, totally ignoring the point of Emily's comment to him.

Not wanting to delve deeper into it, Emily replied, "Just trying to keep you straight."

"Glad you think it's your place to do such a thing!"

"It's a tough job, but somebody's gotta do it." She smiled weakly. "Now come on, we've got a lot to do, and I know just the woman who can help." The two locked arms as they headed over to greet Aunt Louise, whose truck was just pulling into the drive.

CHAPTER THIRTY-ONE

The day of Grace Alderman's funeral was a picture-perfect one with not a cloud in the sky. Luke awoke to the smells of Aunt Louise's pancakes, and for one brief moment, he forgot the events of the past two days and thought it was Sunday morning. The sound of Emily's voice jarred him back to reality, though, and he laid thinking about all that had transpired.

Aunt Louise had met Luke at the Alderman place that Tuesday and brought Emily a change of clothes—she'd gone through her old "skinny" closet, as she called the clothes she could no longer wear, and tried to guess what Emily could and would wear—along with some necessary toiletry items. Of course, Emily had no place to change there, but the extra clothes were the only extra ones she had now, and she was touched by Aunt Louise's thoughtfulness. In fact, Louise didn't realize until she got to the Alderman's how very much she was needed.

Emily relied on Luke and Louise to help her with all the funeral arrangements, and, although John Crawford was there for all the discussions, he neither argued with Emily nor suggested anything different than what she planned. At first, Louise was hesitant to help, feeling that these were all family decisions, and she didn't want to intrude. However, before long, Louise jumped in, adding her opinions and helping Emily with every detail, from picking out the casket to deciding what color dress Grace would wear. Louise wasn't overbearing or controlling. Instead, she was exactly what Emily needed to focus on the tasks at hand and make the tough decisions that faced her.

By the end of the day Tuesday, everyone was exhausted, but no one more than Emily. Aunt Louise had insisted that she stay with Charles, Luke, and her for the next few days, and Emily didn't refuse the offer. At that point, her only other option was her Uncle John, and that would never work.

Visitation was even held at Charles and Louise's on Wednesday evening in lieu of church services, due to the fact that most of the community wanted to pay their respects to Grace's family. Although many were still shocked to hear Grace had been living back in town for some time, and a good many questions were being raised as to why her presence had been kept secret, people still thought a lot of Emily and John Crawford, and they wanted to comfort them as best they could during this difficult time.

The truth about Emily's past and John's treatment of her over the years were put aside for the time being. In a community like Shelby, people came together when bad things happened, no matter who they happened to.

And come together they did. From the time visitation began at 7:00 Wednesday night until way past 10:00, the Garrison house saw a constant stream of neighbors, friends, and a few long-lost relatives of the Alderman family. By the time the last car pulled out of the driveway, it was all Emily could do to make it to the spare bedroom and fall into bed.

Lying there that morning, Luke knew how worn-out he was from the last couple of days, and it was hard for him to imagine Emily already up and helping Aunt Louise with breakfast. Bu since she was, he decided to go ahead and get up, too. He wandered into the kitchen, after throwing on some clothes and found Emily and Louise heavy in conversation. As he entered, the women stopped talking, and Luke felt sure the discussion had been about him. But he was so tired, he didn't really care. Instead, he took a seat at the table and started on a fresh cup of black coffee.

"Morning, ladies," he said, after his first sip of coffee.

Emily smiled but that didn't hide her swollen eyes or the redness in her face. "Hey, sleepyhead—good to see you finally up and at 'em this morning!" she teased.

'What time is it?" he asked. He knew it couldn't be too late because the funeral was scheduled for 1:00, and they would have to be ready way before then. Emily wanted to see her mother prior to the burial, so they would need to leave at least an hour or so before the services in order to go by the funeral home.

Emily and John had both agreed not to have an open casket. The storm had beaten Grace up a little in the face, but that wasn't the real reason. So few people had seen her since JT had died that her appearance would probably be a shock to them. Over the years, Grace had withered away to almost nothing, and Emily and John didn't think the people of Shelby would be able to take it or understand it. So the Wednesday night visitation had only been for Emily and John—there had been no body to view or casket to see.

Emily had also chosen not to have a church service. Instead, there would only be a graveside service. Grace hadn't been to the little country church since before she left to marry Thomas Alderman, and Emily wanted to keep things as short and simple as possible. She knew that's what her mother would have wanted.

"It's almost 10:00; we all slept in this morning, dear," Louise replied.

"Where's Uncle Charles?"

"He's out checking the herd. He's already finished the other chores."

"Oh, man, I'm falling down on my job …"

"Now don't you go worrying about that! If he'd have needed you or wanted you, he could have gotten you up. You needed the rest, Son. It's been a tough couple 'a days."

"Not as tough on me as on Emily. Emily, hon, why didn't you sleep late?" Luke asked, concerned.

Emily shrugged her shoulders. "I don't know. I feel like I'm on my last leg, but when it's time to go to sleep, I can't for the life of me. Or if I do fall asleep, I can't seem to stay that way for long. I tried my darndest to stay still this morning, but by the time 7:00 rolled around, I couldn't lay there any longer."

Louise reached over and squeezed Emily's shoulders. "Now, now, dear, the time will come when you can relax and sleep. Let's just focus on the funeral today, and then you'll have some time to catch back up on your rest."

Emily agreed. "Sounds good to me. I'm just ready for this day to be over with." She came over and sat down beside Luke.

Luke reached for her hand and said, "I think we all are, but just stay focused, and in the next few hours, it'll all be over."

Emily sadly shook her head. "No, Luke, I don't think you understand. It's really only just beginning."

"What do you mean?" Luke probed.

"All right, breakfast is ready—Luke, go call Charles, will ya? Y'all need to eat it while it's hot!"

Luke wanted Emily to answer his question but knew it wasn't the time or place to wait for her reply. Instead, he got up and headed out to find Charles, only to run right into him as he threw open the door at the same time Charles had pulled open the screen door. The two men laughed and simultaneously said, "Breakfast is ready!"

The foursome ate a hearty breakfast while trying to keep the conversation light. Afterwards, Louise quickly cleaned the dishes while Charles, Luke, and Emily headed off to get ready. Louise had found a simple black dress among her "skinny clothes" and had given it to Emily the day before. The dress had fit her perfectly, and Emily had been thrilled. The two had also gone shopping for some black shoes and other essentials Wednesday, so Emily felt good as she began dressing for her mother's funeral. She knew that no matter what happened, her mother would be proud of how she looked today. She just hoped she could hold up to get through it all.

A soft knock on the door startled her. "Emily, are you ready, dear?" It was Louise. "I have a nice set of pearls that will look lovely with that dress."

"Come on in; I'm dressed."

Louise walked in to see Emily more beautiful than she'd ever seen her. She choked back tears as she said, "Emily, you look so much like your mother. You are just so beautiful!"

"Thank you. And thank you for all you've done for me. I can't tell you how much it means to me …"

"Don't you thank me, Honey. I've enjoyed every minute of it, despite the circumstances. You are welcome to stay with us as long as you need to—I hope you know that."

"Yes, ma'am, I do."

Emily turned around and lifted her long hair so Louise could fasten the pearls for her. "They're gorgeous!"

"That's exactly what I was going to say—man, you are gorgeous!" Luke was standing in the doorway.

Emily blushed.

Louise agreed. "That she is. Luke, you know how to pick 'em! Now, are we all ready?"

Emily nodded. "Luke, I was thinking. Could you just drive me to the funeral home?"

"Well, sure, I'd be glad to."

Louise knew what Emily was trying to say. She wanted to see her mother alone, but she didn't want to hurt anyone's feelings, either. Louise chimed in. "You know what? I think that's a great idea. The two of you go ahead, and Charles and I will meet you at the cemetery. That will give me some extra time to get ready. We'll try to get there in time to see you before the service—how does that sound?"

Emily breathed a sigh of relief. Louise had read her mind, and again she was grateful. "That works out wonderfully. Thank you."

Luke nodded. "Well, all right, then. You and I can go on now, if you'd like."

"Sounds good," Emily said. She leaned over and kissed Aunt Louise on the cheek before heading out the door. "See you there."

CHAPTER THIRTY-TWO

The funeral was short and sweet, just as Emily had planned. Mrs. Prescott sang "Amazing Grace," and the pastor preached a short sermon from John 14. The chairs set out by the funeral home were full, and many stood outside the tent as well. Luke, Charles, and Louise sat on the front row with Emily, as did John and Jack Hawkins, and a few of Grace's relatives, although Emily didn't really know any of them all that well. All in all, it was a relief to Emily, John, and even Jack that Grace was finally at peace. After the service, many of the congregation wanted to linger around, catch up with those they hadn't seen lately, and just take their time leaving, but Emily was ready to leave immediately. She'd been gracious the night before at the visitation, and she was ready to put all of this behind her.

She had spent a good half hour with her mother at the funeral home prior to the graveside services. At first, she just looked and observed how beautiful her mother looked, lying there in the pretty pink dress Louise had bought for her to wear. She was an attractive lady, and Emily was pleased at the job the funeral directors had done. She took time to tell her mother how sorry she was for all the grief she had caused. She talked about JT, his death, and all that had transpired since then. It was the first time she'd laid it all out for herself, and she felt a huge burden lifted. She held her mother's hand afterwards and enjoyed the quiet. When she got ready to leave, she knew what she needed to do to close this part of her life and be able to move on to the next. She kissed her mother, told her how much she loved her, and told her goodbye.

Luke had been waiting in the truck for Emily. He was surprised to see her so calm and collected. He had expected that saying her personal goodbye would be the hardest part of all. But when he'd asked her if she was okay, her reply had been, "Better than I've been in a long time. I know now what

I need to do to put the past behind me and move on, but we'll talk about all that another time." Not wanting to pressure her, Luke said nothing. They'd driven in silence to the cemetery, and the service began pretty soon after they arrived.

Now Luke and Emily shared another quiet ride back to the Garrison ranch. Luke wanted to know what Emily meant by what she'd said after leaving the funeral home, but he knew he would have to be patient. Emily had enough to deal with right now; she surely didn't need to deal with his impatience.

Aunt Louise was already getting lunch started as the two arrived back home. Louise told them it would be about thirty minutes before they would eat, so Luke changed clothes and headed out to find his uncle while Emily opted to lie down for a little while. Unbelievably, Emily fell almost immediately into a deep sleep, and when Aunt Louise came in to wake her for lunch, she just didn't have the heart to do it. Emily was sleeping so soundly, and after hearing how she'd had so little rest the past couple of nights, Louise decided to let her sleep.

"She needs the rest more than the food right now," Louise explained to Charles and Luke when the men came in for lunch and noticed Emily's absence. Both agreed and heartily ate their meal before heading back out to the fields. After cleaning up a little, Louise decided to lie down, too, and the house remained quiet for the remainder of the afternoon.

Night fell, supper came and went, and still Emily slept. Several times, Louise went it to check on her, and each time she was sleeping peacefully. It wasn't until the next morning that Emily awoke—rested and extremely appreciative to Louise for not waking her up as they'd discussed before lunch the day before.

CHAPTER THIRTY-THREE

OVER THE NEXT SEVERAL DAYS, EMILY SPENT A great deal of time alone resting and relaxing. She took long walks, rested under the shade trees, and just enjoyed nature's beauty on the Garrison ranch. Luke worried about Emily being alone so much and constantly asked her if she wanted him to stay and be with her, but she always declined the offer. She loved spending time with him, but she had a great deal to think about, and she didn't need her feelings for him clouding her mind.

About a week after her mother's funeral, Emily decided to take care of the little bit of unfinished business she had. She worked for two solid days with her Uncle John, trying to sort through the destruction of her home and salvage the few things that were left. It had been a tough thing to do, but in her mind, each step was a baby step to finally moving on with her life. She confided in her uncle her plans to put the past behind her and start over. He listened and spoke words of encouragement to her, something she'd never heard from him before. Afterwards, she felt that she and her uncle had finally found a way to get along, although she knew they'd never be close. In a way, she felt sorry for him because she knew that he would never move past all that had happened. But that was his choice and his life, and she couldn't make the decisions for him.

Emily also made a trip to the bank to take care of her mother's savings account. The account was one that had been opened when Grace was a child, and it hadn't been accessed by her in years. In fact, the only reason Emily knew about the account was because her Uncle John brought it up. He had asked Emily if Grace still had that account she used to put her earnings in when she worked as a teenager. Emily checked into it and was not only surprised to see that it was still a valid account but that there was a good bit of money in it. She wondered for a moment where that much money had come from but quickly realized there was only one answer to that. So she made another trip—to visit Jack Hawkins.

Jack didn't seem too surprised to see her as he made his way down the steps to meet her in the yard. His voice was gruff and crabby as he greeted her, as if to turn her off from her visit.

"What brings you here?"

Emily wasn't upset or startled by his greeting in the least. Really, she didn't care how he reacted to her, because she was bound and determined not to leave until she found out the answers to her questions.

"I've come to have a little chat with you," she said as she marched past him to the porch and proceeded to take a seat in one of the rocking chairs.

"I didn't invite you to stay," he grumbled.

"And I didn't ask you if I could, now, did I?" Emily snapped. "I have some questions that only you can answer, and I'm not leaving here until you tell me what I need to hear."

"Hmmph, we'll see about that," he retorted, but took a seat in the other rocker anyway.

Emily softened a bit. "Look, Mr. Hawkins, I …"

"It's Jack. Call me Jack."

"Okay, Jack, look, I know that my mother was someone very special to you, and although I don't know …"

"Someone special? She was the love of my life," he choked. "The love of my life."

Emily saw tears in the man's eyes and realized how very much he'd loved her mother. "I'm so sorry. I guess I didn't realize—I'm sorry, Jack."

"It's all right. It's not your fault," he said as he wiped a handkerchief across his eyes.

"Well, I mean, I've always known how you'd help take care of Mama for us while I was working. I knew that. But I guess I just didn't know why."

"I guess it's time to tell you, then. You have a right to know, I reckon. Emily, a long time ago, your mother and I were deeply in love, very deeply in love—until she met your father. It all happened so fast, and I was devastated when she ran off with him. To this day, I still don't know what happened or why it happened. I wonder if, in Grace's mind, it was her only chance to get out of Shelby and find her own way. Then again, Grace was so easily led—she had such a naïve, sweet spirit that could very easily be manipulated, unfortunately. I wonder sometimes if your father was a manipulative type of person who controlled her thinking. I don't know. I just don't know what happened. But I do know that Grace took all those answers to the grave with her, and I'm sorry for that. I honestly wish I could have closure on that area of my life."

"Wow, and after all of that, you still came and took care of her when we moved back here? Why?"

"Because true love never dies, my dear. Oh, sure, I found someone else after Grace, but she never took her place. No one ever took Grace's place in my life or in my heart. Over the years, I thought of her often, and I tried to keep up with her through John. You know, Grace was his life. I've never seen a brother who loved his sister any more than John loved Grace. He hated the fact that she moved away and blamed your father for all of it. I guess, in a way, Grace helped turn two people into hard-hearted, crabby men, although neither of us blames her in the least. We loved her too much for that. Anyway, when your brother died and your father ran out on y'all, John came to me for advice. He didn't know what to do to help, but he knew he needed to do something. I offered to help care for her if he brought her back here, but Jack worried what other people would think of her. We argued over it a good bit—Jack always wanted to protect Grace and worried what others would think of her if they knew she had lost her mind. I, on the other hand, could have cared less what other people thought and just wanted her to be taken care of by those who loved her, no matter what was said behind our backs. Doesn't mean either of us was right. We both loved her. We just had two different opinions as to how to take care of her." He stopped and took a deep breath.

"So, obviously, Uncle John won that argument."

"Well, it was more of a compromise. John agreed to bring her back here for me to help care for her, but I had to promise to keep it a secret. I knew about you and that people would be told that you were living here, but Grace was to be kept a total secret. I agreed because I wanted to be near her so badly. And the days that I was able to stay with her and care for her are some of the best memories I have. Of course, most of the time she talked out of her head and had no idea who I was. But on rare occasions, she would remember—and sometimes, on those special days, she would live in that time period and tell me she loved me, and I would pretend with her. Those memories are something that I will cling to for the rest of my days." He again wiped his eyes. His hands were shaking, but he didn't break down. He was too much of a man for that.

"I appreciate all you did for my mother. I know now how much you loved her, and I am so sorry about your loss."

"As I am for yours," he offered.

"Jack, do you know anything about the money in my mother's savings account?

"Yes, I do."

"Will you tell me about it?"

"I guess you have the right to know about that, too. Years ago, Grace and I talked of getting married and raising our own little family. Grace wanted to open a savings account of her very own. She worked part-time after school, and she tried to save as much money as she could. I told her I had plenty of money and for her not to worry about that, but she was insistent. And whatever Grace wanted, I normally got for her. After a month or so, she began to get frustrated because her money wasn't increasing like she thought it should. So unbeknownst to her, I began adding to it, a little at a time, to help her feelings somewhat. She was so excited about her savings account. She talked about using the money to buy her children the best life had to offer. Then your father came into town, and everything changed. I just assumed the money was gone until a few months after your mother had left town when the lady at the bank stopped me on the street and casually asked me why I hadn't been to see her lately to deposit money into my account. I dismissed the conversation until I got home and really started thinking about it. In my mind, I believed that Grace had left the account open as a window for me that maybe, someday, we'd be back together. So after that, I continued putting money into it, hoping that I was right. And I was—to a certain extent. Anyway, the money was Grace's, and if you use it like she wanted you to, she and I both will be happy."

"Yeah, but it's really your money. I can't spend your money," Emily protested.

"Yes, you can, and you will," Jack countered. "This money was not mine—it was your mother's, and it was her wish that it be used on her children. Being as you're the only child she's got now, it's all yours. Take it and use it wisely."

Emily nodded, not knowing what else to say. Jack patted her hand. "I've led a miserable life, but it's not your mother's fault. I chose to be the mean person I've become. Few people in town like me, and that's from my own doing. I don't have the patience or gumption to go back and try to make things right with all of them, but I'm glad you are going to make something of yourself. Go and be someone Grace will be proud of." He stood up, and Emily realized the visit was over. She had found the answers she needed, and it was time to say goodbye. She leaned over and quickly pecked him on the cheek. Startled, he growled, "What was that for?" although Emily knew he appreciated the gesture.

"It's to say thank you for everything—for loving my mother and taking care of her all these years. It's for saying goodbye and for wishing you all the best in the days to come. Take care, Jack," Emily said as she walked away from the man who probably knew and loved her mother more than anyone else she knew.

When Emily got back from Jack Hawkins' ranch, supper was almost ready, and Luke was just finishing washing up from his work in the fields.

"Hey, Sunshine, where've you been?" Luke asked her.

"Just trying to finish up the rest of Mama's affairs," she replied, heading up the steps and into the house.

"Hey, wait a minute; is there anything I need to help you with?"

Emily shook her head. "Nope, it's all done, thank goodness."

Luke seemed somewhat disappointed. He'd thought Emily would have relied on him more than she had. But ever since the funeral, she'd become a little more confident and less dependent each day. Luke felt a little jealousy creep in, but he didn't know who to be jealous of. He did feel like he was losing her a little, and he didn't know what to do about it. "Say, why don't I take tomorrow afternoon off, and the two of us pack a picnic lunch and spend the afternoon together?"

Emily's eyes lit up. "But what about your uncle? Will he let you?"

Luke grinned. "Oh, I've got my uncle wrapped around my little finger, don't you know that already?"

Emily laughed. "Oh, yeah, I completely forgot that little bit of information!"

Luke chuckled. "Yeah, well, who can resist this puppy-dog look I've got?" He gave her the saddest look he could and waited for her sympathy.

"I can," she countered, laughing. "You aren't going to get any sympathy from me, ol' boy!"

"You wanna bet?" He started after her, and the two were still giggling as they raced inside the house to the kitchen for supper.

"Well, well, what have we here?" Aunt Louise remarked. "Seems the two of you need to share your secret of happiness with the rest of us, ain't that right, Charles?"

"Seems right to me, dear," Uncle Charles added, enjoying the light-hearted atmosphere.

Luke ignored their picking and went straight for what he wanted. "Uncle Charles, is it all right if I take tomorrow afternoon off? I've asked Emily to go on a picnic with me. She told me a few weeks ago that we needed to talk, and I've been patient, but I can't wait any longer. She and I haven't had time together by ourselves in over a week."

"Whoa, whoa—are you trying to convince me or yourself that you need the afternoon off? No reason to give me the scoop! Just go and have a good time. Emily, make sure Louise packs your lunch, though, and not Luke. No telling what that boy might put in there for you to eat!"

"Very funny, Unc! Very funny!" Luke winked at Emily as if to say, "See, I got him wrapped," and Emily was definitely impressed, more so by the love of the Garrison family than anything else. It was as if Luke was Charles and Louise's son, not someone who'd come to stay for just the summer.

After supper and a nice visit on the porch, Emily excused herself to go to bed. She needed some time to think about what she would say to Luke tomorrow about her plans, and she needed the energy and the strength to be strong about her decision. She felt like Luke would try and talk her out of it, but she had to be strong. This was something she had to do, and she wasn't going to let him—or anyone else—stop her.

CHAPTER THIRTY-FOUR

Luke and Emily left for their picnic around 11:00 that next morning. Both of them were excited but nervous as they headed across the pasture to Luke's favorite place on the ranch. It was just on the edge of the Garrison place, with just enough trees to shade the area, but few enough that they would be able to experience the sunset if their afternoon picnic lasted that long—and Luke hoped it would.

As Luke spread out the blanket Aunt Louise had sent with them, Emily began unpacking the picnic basket. Aunt Louise had, of course, packed enough food for an army, and Luke and Emily were thrilled to see she had sent most of Luke's favorite foods, including two huge slices of homemade chocolate cake.

"I don't see where she finds the time to do all she does," Emily remarked.

"I don't, either, but she does. She's one heck of a woman, I'll tell you that!"

Emily agreed. "Luke, what's your mother like? You don't mention her."

Luke replied, "Oh, it's not because I don't miss her. She's a wonderful woman, much like the busy bee Aunt Louise is, but with a little less spark to her. She's more the quiet type—a lot like you, actually. I miss her a great deal, to be honest with you. I've just been so busy this summer, I haven't called her or checked on her as much as I should have. Plus, I guess I needed that time away to get my life in order and move on after my pa's death."

Emily knew this was the window of opportunity for her to tell Luke her plans for the future. "Luke, I'm glad this summer has been good for you. I can see a big difference in you since I first met you, and I'd like to think that I had a small something to do with that."

Luke leaned over and kissed her gently on the lips. "You had a great deal to do with it, my dear. A great deal. I feel like I've grown into the man I'm supposed to be, and that I'm with the woman I'm supposed to be with. And to think it all happened in a couple of months. Some people wait a lifetime …"

"I know," Emily said softly, thinking of Jack Hawkins. "And still others find that person, and for one reason or another, it isn't the right time for them, and they give up ever finding anyone else. Their lives are ruined by one incident, and they never recover."

"Yep, it's sad, all right," Luke commented as he stretched out on the blanket, relaxing a little. "But then there are people like us who find each other as our lives are just beginning. I guess you could say we're the lucky ones."

Emily shifted a little. "Yep, in a way I guess we are. Although I totally believe in second chances, I also believe that you are in control of your own destiny, and you are the one who ultimately decides whether to take the chance or not."

"You and your second chances theory!" Luke kidded.

"I'm not kidding, Luke. Think about it. Every person has opportunities for happiness along the way. Some more than others, of course, but everyone has decisions to make that will affect how his path of life will go. It's all in how a person views himself, the world, and his own destiny that defines who that person is and where his life takes him."

Luke was amazed. "Wow, you've really thought all of this through, haven't you? You haven't been resting this past week; you've been working that brain of yours! I totally agree with you. I've just never thought it all through, that's all."

"I don't know. I think sometimes you don't give yourself enough credit."

"What do you mean?"

"Well," Emily explained, "after your father's death, you made a decision to come here. You felt you needed to get away from things for a while so you could sort everything out, take time to heal, and refocus. Am I right?"

"Yeah, but …"

"Wait, let me finish. You came here and have done exactly that. At the beginning of the summer, you were angry with God and everyone. You couldn't even speak of your father without losing it. But look at you now."

Luke finally began to understand that Emily was trying to tell him something, and it made him nervous. "Emily, where are you taking this?"

Emily slowly pushed her point home. "Luke, I'm having some of the same feelings you did. And I need to act on them—just like you did."

Luke sat up. "What exactly does that mean?" He didn't like the direction the conversation was moving.

"Luke, please try to understand. Just hear me out. After JT died and my father left, my mother immediately began going downhill. Eventually, my Uncle John began making plans to move us back here so Mama could be looked after a little better. In the process, I lost track of my father. I put all of it in the back of my mind because it was easier; and, well, I still had my mother, for the most part. But now that she's gone, the only family I have left is my father. And I have no idea where he is."

Luke took her hand. "Sometimes things just work out that way. You do have me, you know."

"I know I do. But listen to me. When I was at the funeral home, I took the time to sit and actually listen to my heart. And it made me realize once and for all what I have to do to be able to get beyond all that's happened."

"But I thought you were moving on—with me," Luke protested.

"Luke, honey, you're not listening to me." Emily was trying her best to explain herself, but Luke was putting up a wall to protect himself from getting hurt. "Luke, I'm not trying to break things off with you. I'm just saying that I need to take some time for closure. I've been working on closing things here, and I feel comfortable, for the most part, that I've done that. But I still have that open part of my life that needs my attention. I need to go back to South Georgia and see if I can locate my father. I want to spend some time with him, get to know him, and try to understand why he left us. Otherwise I'll always ask myself 'why' or 'what if?' And I don't think I can fully move on with my life until I can make total sense of my past."

Luke didn't want to understand, but he did nonetheless. And as hard as it was for him, he had to respect her for what she wanted to do. "I think you are doing the right thing," he finally said, struggling to get all the words out.

Surprised, Emily asked, "You do? But I thought …"

"Look, Emily. Obviously you've spent a lot of time thinking about this. I mean, I know how I felt about coming here. It wasn't just something I wanted to do, but something I needed to do—for me. I can't sit here and tell you that I'm happy you are going away for a while, but I can't try and stop you, either, because I think you are doing what you need to do."

Emily reached out and hugged Luke hard. Then she took a deep breath. She was relieved that the tension had eased off and that Luke was actually being supportive of her. The worst was over.

"When are you planning to leave?"

"Tomorrow."

He wasn't prepared for her response, and he pulled back from her embrace. *"Tomorrow?"*

"Well, I don't think waiting around here will make things better, because the more time I spend with you, the harder it will be for me to leave."

"I suppose. 'Course, I could always go with you," he suggested.

She disagreed. "You and I both know that this is something I need to do on my own. Plus, you need to be here to help your uncle. And who knows how long I'll be? The end of the summer is near, and you'll be headin' back to Bozeman soon."

Luke didn't want to think about all of that right now. He couldn't imagine going back to Bozeman without Emily—but more importantly, he couldn't imagine being in Shelby without her, either. "So, you don't know how long you'll be gone? A month? Maybe two?"

"I don't know, Luke. Once I get to Ocilla, I'll have to ask around for help locating my father. I have relatives there, but it's been so long, I don't know if I can remember their names and faces that well. Hopefully it will be easy to find him. But it may not be. Either way, I'm there until I find him, no matter how long it takes."

"I guess we'll just have to be long distance for a while, huh?"

"Yep, but it won't last forever—don't give up on me!"

"Oh, I won't—I want my second chance with you!" The two held each other for a while, and then ate their picnic lunch. Neither wanted the afternoon to end, so they stayed until way past sunset, eating their lunch leftovers for supper and basking in the glory of the night sky. It was a romantic time together, but a sad one, too, as they both knew it would be a long time before they would be together again.

The next morning, Emily broke the news to Charles and Louise over breakfast. The two were not surprised, but they were definitely disappointed that Emily's short visit with them was already coming to an end.

Louise helped Emily gather the few belongings she had while Charles pulled her truck around. Emily's uncle had offered for Emily to drive his truck since hers was neither dependable nor capable of making the long road trip. At first, Emily was skeptical as to why her uncle was offering to help her, but then she realized that Grace's death was a step toward closure for John as well, and she had accepted his offer. She would make the switch in town after she stopped at the bank to make her withdrawal. Luke and Charles both offered her money, but she wouldn't take it. She didn't go into a lot of detail as to why, but she did tell them that her mother had left some savings for her and that she would be okay.

She hugged Charles and Louise and told them how much she appreciated everything the two had done for her. "Thank you both for everything," she told them. "I love you both very much, and I hope to see you again real soon." Louise wiped tears from her eyes, and Charles led her slowly back into the house.

Luke grabbed Emily and hugged her tightly. "I-I don't want t-to let you go," he stammered.

"I know." Emily held back tears. "This is one of the hardest things I've ever had to do, but you and I both know it needs to be done."

"Be careful, please."

"I will. I'll write as soon as I know where I'll be staying. I may even have a chance to call. We'll just have to take it one day at a time."

"I love you, Emily," Luke said as he leaned down to kiss her.

"I love you, too," she said as their lips brushed against each other. It was a gentle kiss that became more passionate, as if they knew it would be the last kiss between them. Neither wanted it to end, but eventually Emily pulled away, breathless.

"I—I gotta go. If I don't, I never will," she cried. She was sobbing as she climbed into her truck, but she didn't let that stop her. As she pulled out of the driveway, she looked back in her rearview mirror. The last image she saw of Luke was him wiping his own tears away.

CHAPTER THIRTY-FIVE

Luke got up from his rocking chair and stepped off the porch. The storm had not been as fierce as the weatherman had predicted, and he'd ridden it out daydreaming in his porch rocker. A lot had happened since that summer with Emily. It had been thirty years since he'd allowed himself to delve that deeply into his past. Although he'd allowed himself to think of Emily every now and then, this had been the first time he'd let himself reminisce to the fullest extent.

Emily had left that summer to find her father in Georgia, and she'd been successful in her search. Luke had left Shelby, too, not long after Emily left, to go back home to Bozeman. Luke remembered hearing from Emily several times over the first few months she was gone. Her letters and calls were always chock full of information about her search and how she'd found her father, and then eventually how the two of them were slowly reconnecting.

Her stay in Georgia was prolonged on several occasions, and her letters and phone calls became more sporadic and unpredictable. Over time, Luke knew in his heart that he was losing Emily, but she was finding herself—and that was more important to him. His love for her couldn't deny her that opportunity.

Luke, of course, was devastated, but he ultimately made the decision to be a better person because of his experiences and not become bitter or disheartened. He'd seen what that could do to people, and he didn't want to become like John Crawford or Jack Hawkins. In his mind, his time with Emily would have meant absolutely nothing if he didn't take it and learn from it.

So he did. He dove into his work, totally taking over his father's ranch, gradually expanding the entire operation. He became a dedicated church member and was there for every Sunday and Wednesday night service, just as his Aunt Louise had taught him. And, of course, he was a devoted son who took care of his mother with the love and patience of a gentle and kind man.

Then, one day, in the midst of his daily living—and really when he least expected it—he met a wonderful woman named Sarah who eventually won his heart. Sarah and Luke made a comfortable life together, raising two boys and making a healthy living for themselves on the very ranch Luke had grown up on.

Looking back at it all, Luke smiled. He truly believed he'd led a good life, and he had no regrets. He would never forget Emily, and one day he may even look for her again. But right now he was content. He had spent many happy years with a woman who had adored him and was a terrific mother to his kids. Sarah had been what he needed, and in some strange way he felt that he should thank Emily for that. Not really because she didn't return, but because in some strange way, Emily helped him realize that Sarah was the woman he should settle down with. It happened after Luke and Sarah had been dating for a while and the two became involved in a rather serious discussion about life and love. After a pause in the conversation, Sarah cocked her head toward Luke and asked him this question: "So tell me, Luke, do you believe in second chances?"

ACKNOWLEDGEMENTS

Momma and Daddy, thank you for your unconditional love, guidance, and Christian upbringing. I am so blessed to have you as parents. I love you.

Chad – you are my big brother, business associate, hero, and friend. I don't know if I ever told you, but I prayed for God to give me a son first so my future daughter(s) could have what I always had with you. I love you.

Melanie – you are my sister, best friend, confidante, and partner in crime. I will forever cherish our nightly ritual – GNILYSTSDSYITMST YBMOISTYBAOITYTYWYWTYTGN – I love you.

Papa and Grandmama -- you filled my childhood full of fun! You spoiled me rotten, and I have loved every minute of it! I love you.

Kaitlyn, Casen, Cameron, Anna Leigh, and Sarabeth – I love each one of you so much!! I am so proud to be your Aunt Andi!

Jason and Leigh – you became part of the Sumner family because of marriage, but we became friends because we wanted to be. And, I am a better person because of your friendship. I love you.

Granny, Pappy, Redonna, Ken, Susan, and Dill – thank you for making me part of your family – I love you.

And to all those who have helped shape my life in some small way – thank you! In some shape or form, you have helped formulate this book. If I start to list names, I would most likely leave out an important one. Please know, however, that each of you have touched my heart and I am forever grateful. *"I thank my God upon every remembrance of you." Philippians 1:3*

Breinigsville, PA USA
19 January 2010
230984BV00003B/2/P

9 781615 070411